Colin deliberately didn't think about the attack as he escorted Mia home.

She hadn't mentioned any details, and if she'd seen anything as outrageous as fangs or glowing eyes, she'd likely put it down to her imagination. After all, no sane person believed that vampires really existed.

When they reached Mia's gate, Colin let her go, but the gesture turned into a caress down the length of her arm. He was too aware of her shiver, and the way her skin heated at his touch. His own breath caught as desire curled through him.

They both took a quick step back. Colin's fingers slowly reached to touch her cheek without conscious volition, but at the last moment, she turned her head.

"Go away," she said, her voice tight and barely audible. "Just go away."

* * *

"Susan Sizemore enraptures readers,
securing her rightful place among
the writers who will soon rise to the top."
—*Romantic Times*

I Hunger for You is also available as an eBook.

Praise for *I Burn for You*

"With her new twist on ancient vampire lore, Sizemore creates an excellent and utterly engaging new world. *I Burn for You* is sexy, exciting, and just plain thrilling. It's the perfect start for a hot, new series."
—*Romantic Times*

"I adored *I Burn for You* and really hope it's the beginning of another wonderful vampire series from Ms. Sizemore."
—*Old Book Barn Gazette*

"Sizemore has long worn two writing hats, that of romance author and sf-fantasy scribe, and . . . the bonding of [her] two literary worlds is as powerful as what Alex and Domini feel for each other in this sexy read laced with laughter, the first in a burning new series."
—*Booklist*

"Sizemore's hunky vamps can visit me anytime! I was so sorry to see this book end. This one is a must-buy."
—*All About Romance Review*

I Thirst for You

A Pocket Star Book published by
POCKET BOOKS, a division of Simon & Schuster, Inc.
1230 Avenue of the Americas, New York, NY 10020

This book is a work of fiction. Names, characters, places and incidents are products of the author's imagination or are used fictitiously. Any resemblance to actual events or locales or persons, living or dead, is entirely coincidental.

ISBN-13: 978-1-4165-2355-0
ISBN-10:   1-4165-2355-3

This Pocket Star Books paperback edition April 2006

10 9 8 7 6 5 4 3 2 1

POCKET STAR BOOKS and colophon are registered trademarks of Simon & Schuster, Inc.

Cover art by Tom Hallman

Manufactured in the United States of America

For information regarding special discounts for bulk purchases, please contact Simon & Schuster Special Sales at 1-800-456-6798 or business@simonandschuster.com.

I Hunger for You

SUSAN SIZEMORE

POCKET STAR BOOKS

NEW YORK   LONDON   TORONTO   SYDNEY

For Scott Ham—
who can be clever and inspiring
even while driving in heavy traffic

Chapter One

"The suspects finally answered the phone. Looks like we have a robbery gone sour. Maybe we can work with their demands."

The negotiator's voice, heard through Colin Foxe's headset, sounded relieved.

"Do you want us to hold?" Colin's team leader questioned.

After a considerable pause, the negotiator said, "Get your team in place, but wait for a go."

There was already an officer down inside; a cop who'd noticed something suspicious while driving by. She'd called it in, then gone inside. Shots had been fired. The situation escalated quickly after that, and now Colin's SWAT team was on the ground and on the move.

He could smell the wounded officer's blood through a bullet hole in the window. He could also sense the faint flutter of her heartbeat. She wasn't dead, but she didn't have much time. He couldn't see inside, since curtains had been pulled across the wide windows at the front of the office building, but he could sense a tangled mixture of physical markers and high emotions.

It was everybody on the team's job to stop this situation, but Colin took it very personally. He'd taken vows to protect and serve humanity that were far stronger and more binding than even his oath as a Los Angeles police officer.

He and his SWAT team were here to see that the hostages and injured cop were saved. It was a great team, well trained, well coordinated, well led; he was proud to be a part of it.

Dressed entirely in black, he moved in line with the rest of the team. Crouching low, they formed in a loose circle that was stealthily closing in on the one-story building. Their target was a small publishing company located in an office park on a quiet side street. There were at least four armed men inside, holding a dozen hostages.

The cloudy night covered the team's movements. They used nightscope goggles to focus on their objective—all but Colin, who'd perched his on the brim of his helmet. He could see in the dark.

Though he was outwardly calm, the excitement of the hunt burned through him. He was *aware*, the extra senses he reined in much of the time now fully focused. He could smell fear, and taste it as well. The threat of violence hung around the office building like a pall of smoke. And one touch of anger scratched across his senses like nails on slate.

He didn't think the fury was coming from one of the perps. It was one of the hostages, and she—yes, that was definitely a strong sense of femaleness— she was royally pissed off. In a hostage situation, it was better to be scared than angry. Scared people were more likely to keep their heads down and do as they were told, increasing their chances of survival. Colin didn't like this; it added risk to the situation. If this woman did something stupid . . .

Telepathy wasn't his strongest sense, and using it might distract him from the team effort. Besides, there were far too many people with heightened senses inside for him to affect one individual. Still, he risked sending one thought toward perps and hostages alike.

Calm down.

I am calm, came the immediate reply.

It took all his training to keep him from surging out of his crouch in surprise. She heard him! And answered! And the brief touch of her mind on his made him red-hot.

Shouts erupted from the building, followed by shots. And screams.

"Go!"

He was up and moving even as the command came.

He was the first one through the door, rushing in just in time to see the flying side kick that knocked away the gun of the man who would have shot him.

"Hey!" Colin shouted at the woman who'd disarmed the shooter.

"Thanks for the distraction." Then she jumped and kicked again, straight up, taking the bad guy under the chin. He dropped like a rock.

Colin grabbed her by the waist as she came back down, and pushed her to the floor.

"Stay put," he ordered, as the rest of his team came boiling in through the door he'd broken down.

Big brown eyes looked up at him, full of shock and fury that sizzled all the way through him. He pointed for her to get under a nearby desk, then turned and took out another gunman. There was already a third man down; no doubt the Karate Kid had gotten him. Which was probably why the shooting had started.

Farther back, in the rooms beyond this reception area, he heard shouts and screaming. Members of the team were heading that way at a run. A medical team was already working on the injured cop; others were cuffing the downed men.

"You could have gotten everybody killed!" Colin yelled at the woman.

"Well, I didn't!" she shouted back.

This was no time for an argument. Colin quickly rejoined his team and got into the well-practiced rhythm of a rescue operation. But even as he helped to secure the rest of the bad guys, part of him was still aware of the impression of soft, warm flesh over hard muscle that he'd gotten in the moment he held her. Her skin held the scent of ginger and her psychic signature was pure heat, as if her blood was laced with chili peppers.

He couldn't let it go. He marched back to the front of the building as soon as the whole place was secure. By now she was out from under the desk, and one of the medics was arguing with her. Colin noticed that one side of her face was badly bruised, and she was cradling her left hand with her right.

Anger shot through him, and a hot, possessive protectiveness. "Who hurt you?" he demanded.

She looked around, and her dark brown eyes locked on his. "I'm fine."

"That doesn't answer the question."

Her gaze flickered to an unconscious perp on the floor, then back to Colin. "I took care of it."

Her response only served to redirect his annoyance at her. He ripped off his helmet and headset to glare at her fully. "You had no business doing what you—"

"Hey!" She interrupted him. "I saved your ass."

"No, you didn't."

"He was going to shoot you when you came through that door."

"He wouldn't have." Colin took the woman by the shoulders and was instantly and intimately aware of the warmth of her skin. "My job is to do the rescuing."

Her anger was incandescent. "You were a little late. Those men held us hostage for four hours. Where were you?"

"Organizing a *safe* rescue." Everything about her burned him, but he liked it. She infuriated him, needed to be tamed, and he liked that, too.

"Did you stop at Starbuck's for a few hours on the way?" She jerked her head to where the medics were working on the wounded officer. "She could have died. We all could have. Somebody had to do something."

"So you took it upon yourself to play hero? Bad move, sister."

Her head came up sharply, brown eyes flashing. He could have kissed her then and there. "I am not your sister."

"And you're no hero, either," Colin shot back.

"Officer," the medic cut in. He put a hand firmly on Colin's arm. "Officer."

The Prime part of Colin almost turned on the medic with bared fangs, as if the man was challenging him for a mate. It shocked him that the instinctive impulse was nearly triggered by a mortal, and it took him a moment to get the vampire part of himself under control. He had to close his eyes, take a deep breath—and let the woman go.

"Ms. Luchese's injured," he heard the medic say. "We need to get her to the ER."

"I told you I'm fine," she said.

This reminded Colin that a few moments ago, his impulse had been to make someone pay for hurting her. He looked at her and said, "Luchese, you always think you know best, and never do what you're told, right?"

She smiled. It was wicked and edgy, and that lit a different kind of fire in him.

"Yeah," she acknowledged.

"Go with the medic," he told her. She would have protested further, but he sent a stern command into her mind. *Go.*

Then his team commander called him, and Colin went back to work.

Several hours later, he met the Luchese woman in the ER waiting room as she came out of a treatment room. There were plenty of cops around, making his presence fairly anonymous in the hub-bub, so it didn't look like he was hanging around waiting for her. Yet she spotted him instantly, as if she was as drawn to him as he was to her. He watched her look at him, then look away. He felt her consider walking past him and out the door. Her left arm was in a sling, and a shiny cream covered the bruises on her face. Her shoulders had a tired slump to them, which she consciously straightened when she saw him. Apparently she was ready to do battle all over again.

"You look beautiful," he said, coming up to her.

Her eyes went wide in surprise. She clearly thought he was making fun of her, and asked, "Officer, are you supposed to talk like that?"

"I'm off duty."

"You're not here to—take a statement, or something?"

"Didn't an officer talk to you already?"

"Yeah. He told me everyone got out okay. But why are you—"

"I wanted to check on you." He couldn't help but run a hand up her uninjured arm. He felt her shiver. "How are you feeling?"

"Nothing's broken, just a sprained wrist," she answered. "I don't need the sling, but I promised the nice intern who looked at it that I'd wear it until I'm outside the hospital door." She took a deep breath, and made a wry face. "I'm sorry I yelled at you. You risked your life to save us. Thank you."

He gave a slight shrug, and refrained from telling her that she shouldn't have risked her life when he was there to take care of her kind. Mortal life was precious; it was an honor to protect the helpless— even if Luchese here didn't think she was.

"I was scared," she went on. "That made me—testy."

"What were you doing out in the front office with your captor? Why weren't you tied up in the back with the others?"

"I thought you weren't here to ask questions?"

"Not officially. I'm curious. You were up to something, weren't you?"

"They were making ransom demands," she answered. "They were incompetent idiots with guns. They—"

"Had the wrong building," he filled in. "We know that from questioning them. By the time they figured out they'd screwed up, the officer had called the robbery in. But what were you doing?"

"Trying to split them up, so I could take one down and get his weapon. They were demanding a lot of money, and threatening to kill people if they didn't get it. So I said I was an heiress, and if they'd let me call my family, they'd be rich. I got one of them to take me up front so I could use the receptionist's phone, while one of the others was occupied talking to your negotiator in the back. It worked." She laughed, but the sound was a little shaky. "And I was only there to pick up my friend Courtney for lunch."

He shook a finger under her nose. "Luchese, that was very stupid of you. But brave," he added, as a flash of annoyance went through her. He touched the tip of her nose, then found himself tracing the outline of her lips. Soft, full, warm lips. They sent a wave of hunger through him. He was going to kiss those lips soon. The smoldering look she gave him told him he knew it, too. He was going to taste her. But this was not the place.

He made himself take a step back. "My name's Colin Foxe," he finally introduced himself. "You have a first name, Luchese?"

"Mia," she answered. "Mia Luchese."

Mia. A short, pretty, uncomplicated mortal name. It had nothing in common with the complex, beautiful names of vampire females. Someday he was going to bond with a vampire female, but right now he wanted this human woman.

He reached out and took her uninjured hand. "I'll take you home."

Chapter Two

Six months later

It wasn't true that he came here every night.

Only the nights when he wasn't on duty, or when sex with anyone else was out of the question, or when he was in town. All right, he came here a lot—but that didn't mean he was a stalker.

He certainly wasn't in love; it wasn't an emotional attachment. It was just a physical thing, a visceral thing, a psychic residue messing him up.

In fact, Colin was furious—with himself, and with her—because he hadn't yet been able to let it go.

It was just an ache. He'd go so far as to admit to an obsession. A short-term one.

He got hard just thinking about her, and her scent on the air drove him mad. Occasionally he caught a stray thought or emotion at a distance, and that was worse. Even such accidental intrusion was wrong. The memory of the taste of her kisses, and of her skin—hard muscles beneath ginger-scented, satiny flesh—was torture.

But he knew he'd get over it.

All it needed was time, and detachment, and making love to enough other women to drown the memories of how sweet it was with *her*. He refused to give in to the call to go to her. It had nothing to do with respecting her feelings, and everything to do with mastering his own. Wanting Mia Luchese was an obsession he would master. He was stronger than she was.

So Colin stood here, across the street from her place one more time, looked at her house perched on a hillside above Coldwater Canyon, and fought the compulsion. He'd beat it. Get over her. Get on with his life.

She was mortal. If nothing else, he'd outlive the object of his desire. She'd get old, and die, and he'd go on—without her.

"Oh, goddess!"

The first month hadn't been so bad. She'd picked up and left town, no doubt researching articles for travel and extreme sports magazines. Even without the writing, Mia could afford to go when and where she pleased. It turned out what she'd told the perps about being an heiress was true. Colin remembered how he'd found out.

The balcony off her bedroom was small, hardly more than a perch with a wrought-iron rail, but it was perfect for looking at the spectacular view. It was a little past midnight, with a cool breeze drying the sweat on their skins, and a full moon high overhead. To him it was as bright as day, and Mia was beautiful by moonlight, her creamy skin bathed in silver.

He'd come to her straight from a very tough operation. Someone had died, and it hadn't been one of the bad guys. He'd needed her, and she'd taken him to her bed. The sex had been frantic, cathartic, wonderful.

Now they were out on the balcony, pressed so closely together, naked skin to naked skin, that he couldn't tell where he stopped and she started. His hands were around her waist; her head was tilted back, resting on his chest while she looked at the moon. He felt her trying to think of something to say or do, to keep his mind from going over and over what had gone wrong.

He welcomed the distraction, and helped her out by asking, "What are you doing living in a house like this?" The Spanish-style house wasn't big but it was very nice, with a pool and a half-acre of gardens surrounded by a high stucco wall.

He knew she was a freelance writer, but she also spent much of her time practicing a lot of dangerous, physically demanding hobbies. She ran, she was into karate and kung fu; she liked target shooting, and competed in traditional archery. She'd told him about the skydiving, the snowboarding; they'd gone rock climbing together. She was female, but not at all soft.

He liked that she shared some of his interests, and that she competed hard even if he never quite let her win. Competent or not, Mia was a mortal woman, and he wouldn't encourage over-confidence even if she was never likely to be in danger again.

She was a major jock, and being a jock on the level Mia practiced took not only time, but money. He'd made sure they didn't have many personal conversations. He listened to whatever she chose to tell him, but he didn't ask, and he never volunteered anything. He'd kept everything in the present tense, because vampires had to guard their privacy, and because he wasn't planning on staying. The less he knew about her out of bed, the better. He shouldn't be prying into her personal life now, but he was suddenly curious.

"I inherited this place," Mia answered. "The house belonged to my grandmother. It's one of the things she bought when she finally reconciled with her father."

"Reconciled?"

"Long, sad story. I've heard a lot about him, and about his side of the family, but I've never met the old man. He left my great-grandmother when Grandma was a kid. I hear that my great-grandfather's richer than God, and has a few years on Him, as well. Grandma was middle-aged, with kids and a perfectly good life, when a lawyer brought her a letter and a check from her long-lost dad. Grandma didn't use much of the guilt money he dumped on her for herself, but she invested wisely, and left fortunes to my sister and me."

"So, you have a fairy grandfather—"

"Great-grandfather, and he's more of a—" Mia shrugged, and desire shot through Colin as he felt the movement all along his body.

He moved his hands up from her waist to her lovely, round breasts and—

He remembered the sex now—her sharp gasp of pain and pleasure when he sank teeth into flesh; the way the world turned to fire when he entered her—and it was far more vivid and important than any memory of conversation. It wasn't who she was, but how Mia made him feel that drew him to her like an addiction. He didn't understand what she'd done to him.

It wasn't as if he'd taken much blood from her.

He'd done his best to keep the psychic connection between them as tenuous as possible. He'd only wanted her as a bed partner.

He *still* wanted her.

He'd known when she'd returned, knew the instant she was back in L.A. He'd dismissed the knowledge as his imagination, and hadn't given in to the impulse to just drive by her house for another month. But here it was, three months after the end of a three-month affair, and things were getting worse instead of better. He sure as hell hoped she was heartbroken and emotionally devastated, because he didn't want to be alone in this hell.

But she was mortal, a brief candle, a butterfly, a bright burst of fireworks—lovely, warm, and exciting—but ephemeral. How long could something as finite as a mortal creature feel hurt?

She was doubtless over him. In fact, someone as passionate as Mia had probably had at least one lover since they parted.

The very thought of Mia in anyone else's bed set his fangs on edge, and hit him like a hard punch in the gut. But he told himself it was only because Primes were proprietary. He'd unconsciously marked her as his, which was what this returning here night after night was about. It was a sort of instinct.

It's really good practice, he told himself. This pallid obsession was a way of preparing for the extreme emotions inevitable when the opportunity for a true bonding with a female of his own kind came his way.

In the meantime—

Thoughts of the future disappeared abruptly, and Colin's whole body tensed as Mia's garden gate opened across the street. Pounding need drove through him when he saw her step away from the gate. For a moment she was illuminated under the glow of a streetlight, wearing a red tank top and shorts that showed off her toned body. While she was poised like a pop singer under a bright spotlight, Colin couldn't help but take a step forward, his hands stretched toward her.

She was unaware of him, of course. His kind had a knack for using shadows to their advantage, blending into darkness as if it was their natural coloration. If he tried, he could use his other senses to measure her heartbeat, the temperature of her skin. Her scent was alive on the breeze. When she turned and began to run, he beat down the hunter's instinct to follow.

She's exercising, you fool! She was a normal mortal, doing normal mortal things. He had no business being here, let alone pursuing her. He threw his head back, bumping it against the bark of the palm tree under which he stood. No business being here at all.

So he began to walk—not back to where he'd parked his car, but the way Mia had gone. He was *not* following her—he was just stretching his legs.

Mia didn't normally go running on the streets, especially this late, but something about the night had called out to her. The walls of the house had made her feel claustrophobic, and she needed space. Restlessness clawed at her. Surfing the Net hadn't helped; watching television hadn't held her attention; listening to a book tape while using the treadmill had bored her. She'd thought about calling her girlfriend Courtney, but her mind was too much on Foxe, and any conversation would only degenerate into another bitching session about "that jerk." Why go over that ground again, when she was trying to forget him? She must have bored her friends to death with the subject by now—she wasn't the suffering-in-silence type.

I'm not suffering, she told herself as she eased her body into the rhythm of running. It was just that sometimes it felt like he was nearby, like she could reach out and touch him, and then—

Then she'd wake up from a dark, erotic dream, and be alone in her bed, and all the sexual energy was still there, simmering—

It was bound to wear off eventually. She'd meet someone else. Life would go on.

Some nights were just worse than others, and this was one of them. Mia figured all she had to do was drive herself to exhaustion; then she could fall asleep without dreaming. So she ran.

Except for the occasional passing car, the street was empty. The sidewalk was clear of pedestrians. There were lights in a few houses, but the neighborhood was mostly dark. Too dark, she thought after a while, and way too quiet.

A sensation of dread began to creep into Mia's consciousness, a feeling that she was being watched, even stalked. That something *wanted* her to be out here. It wasn't anything tangible. She didn't see or hear anything out of the ordinary, though she slowed down and looked around carefully. It was just *there*.

She turned around and headed back home. She trusted her instincts, even if there was no evidence. She knew she was being hunted. She didn't know if making it back to her house would mean making it to safety, but making it home was the only goal she could reach for as she ran through the darkness.

And it was getting darker. It was a cloudless night, but the stars seemed to be fading. Each streetlight she passed seemed dimmer than the last. She couldn't make out any lights in the houses; in fact she couldn't even see the houses anymore. The trees and bushes lining the sidewalk became dark, menacing shadows.

Then the darkness *moved*, resolved into a man-shaped shadow. She thought she caught a glimpse of bright, glowing eyes. The apparition reached for her with pale, clawed hands.

Colin was running even before he heard her angry shout up ahead. He cursed himself for not noticing the depth of the darkness sooner—that it had solidity, weight, and menace—for not noticing that there was another vampire in the area.

Motion swirled inside the darkness that spread like a scrim across the sidewalk. Emotion swirled as well, and Colin recognized more than just Mia's shock and controlled fear. She was putting up a fight. Like a cat playing with prey, the other vampire projected fierce joy at her puny efforts to kick and punch her way out of trouble. No Clan or Family Prime would take his pleasure like that.

"Tribe." Colin breathed the word as a curse as he sped forward.

It felt as if he had to rip through a curtain covering his mind, but he came through it at a rush to find the pair locked in combat in the small space between a tall hibiscus hedge and a parked SUV. Colin caught a brief impression of Mia twirling and kicking, and the vampire's preternaturally swift feint. The Tribe vampire's light hair was worn in a long braid that hung down his back and swayed as he moved, silver in the moonlight.

Colin grabbed the thick braid and used it to haul the Tribe Prime away from Mia. The Tribe spun around, showing a mocking grin, and fangs bared in challenge. When the other Prime grabbed his braid and tugged, Colin let it go.

"Run!" he called to Mia, and barreled forward to grab the Tribe around the waist and forcibly haul him through a narrow gap in the hedge.

The Tribe fought his way out of Colin's grasp, deeply clawing Colin's arms to do so.

"Scared to fight in front of a girl?" the Tribe asked when they faced each other again.

Colin's own claws and fangs were out by now. He sneered, and gestured the white-haired vampire forward.

The Tribe laughed, and they crouched and circled, taking on the ritual movements of two

Primes fighting over possession of a female. Fangs and claws flashed, bodies moved at lightning speed. Blows were struck and avoided. The object was to draw blood.

On the other side of the hedge, Mia shouted, "What's going on? I'm calling the cops!"

Why hadn't the fool woman run?

"I am the cops!" Colin yelled back.

"What the—Colin, is that you?"

"She doesn't sound happy to see you," the Tribe sneered.

The mockery infuriated Colin, but he didn't let it distract him. He lunged forward, and this time he got under the other vampire's guard. Colin's claws raked across the Tribe's smirking face, leaving four thin lines of blood across his cheek.

The Prime howled and leaped away. He disappeared into the waning night within moments, though cold laughter echoed back out of the darkness. Tribe Primes weren't known for their honor, but this one seemed to abide by the rules of mating challenge, accepting defeat at the loss of first blood.

Colin's first impulse was to howl in victory and take possession of his prize—who was on the other side of the bushes. The emotions emanating from her were anything but simpering delight in having been defended by a champion Prime of Clan Reynard. He'd made the decision that she would never know about vampires when they first met, and he fought off the impulse to change his mind now.

Colin closed his eyes and took a few moments to calm down. He shook from adrenaline and need, but he balled his fists and wouldn't move. His body screamed at him that he was crazy—she was so very close—he should drag her down on the grass and take her!

"Colin!"

"Go!" he shouted.

Mia stuck her head through the gap in the hedge, framing her face in hibiscus blossoms. "What are you doing here?"

He'd managed to draw in his fangs and claws just in time. He slapped his mental shields in place, not wanting to give in to what he felt. He didn't want to know what she felt, either, not in the vivid way of his kind.

He stepped forward, relentlessly making her move backward until they were both back on the sidewalk. He could sense the racing of her heart.

He put a hand on her arm. As dangerous as it was to touch her, he kept hold of her and made her walk with him toward her house. "I told you to get out of here, Luchese."

"What are you doing here, Foxe?" she repeated.

"Saving your ass—as usual."

"I was doing fine before you showed up."

"I've heard that before."

"You're the one who could have been—"

"Could have been what?" he demanded when she bit off her words.

She shook her head. "Shouldn't you be chasing the bad guy?" she countered. "Officer."

"I will, after I escort you home. Ma'am."

"That isn't necessary."

"No. But I think I left some CDs at your place," he offered as an excuse. "I stopped by to see if you had them."

"Anything you might have left, I burned, or used as target practice."

"That's fair enough."

Colin glanced at the sky as they walked. Dawn wasn't that far off. Most Tribe Primes made a point of perverse pride in not taking the daylight drugs that allowed Primes like Colin to emulate mortal existence. Mia would be safe from dawn until dusk. And by nightfall, Colin would have tracked down the Tribe scum who had dared to try to touch her. He'd have to inform the local Matri and elders right away that at least one Tribe was playing the old games in Clan territory; then he could get on with his own hunt.

He would not love this woman, but he would protect her.

It was his fault the Tribe Prime had chosen her as a victim. Though Colin hadn't shared his blood with Mia, they had shared an intense physical relationship. Though she wasn't aware of it, Mia was psychic, and they had sometimes touched on that level, as well. The residue of that sharing was what kept Colin coming back over and over, while he waited for the connection to fade.

That residue must also have been sensed by the Tribe Prime. In the old days, when the Clans, Families, and Tribes fought one another, the Tribes counted coup by stealing mortal lovers from Clan or Family enemies. The world was supposedly a safer and more peaceful place for vampires these days, but the Tribes were still vicious, unpredictable bastards.

And it was going to be a pleasure to kill the one who'd attacked Mia.

Mia drew more in on herself with each step, her silence stubborn and angry. She would not glance his way. She suffered his touch, but tried to pretend he wasn't even there. She certainly didn't want him there.

He deliberately didn't talk about the attack. She hadn't mentioned any details about it, and if she'd seen anything as outrageous as fangs or glowing eyes, she'd likely put it down to her imagination or stage makeup. After all, this was Hollywood, where anything was possible. And no sane person believed that vampires really existed.

When they reached her gate, he let her go, though the gesture automatically turned into a caress down the length of her arm. He was too aware of her shiver, and the way her skin heated at his touch. His own breath caught as desire curled through him. They both took a quick step back. His fingers slowly reached to touch her cheek without conscious volition, but at the last moment, she turned her head away.

"Go away," she said, voice tight and barely audible. "Just go away."

It hurt to hear the words, far more than he thought it could. But he could do nothing but obey her. After all, it was what he wanted, as well.

Mia couldn't breathe for a few moments because of the tears that choked her throat.

How dare the gorgeous bastard show up and save her life again?

She fumbled at the latch, and nearly fell through to the other side when it opened. She slammed it behind her as hard as she could. The wrought-iron gate shrieked on its hinges, and bounced back to hit her on the wrist.

She welcomed the sharp pain. It helped clear her head of everything but the memory of his touch, the cocky confidence in the way he moved, the dark red hair that framed his angular face, the heavy arch of eyebrows over the darkest eyes in the world, the way she missed his body covering hers, the sound of his voice, the heat of his kisses.

The way he'd left her for no reason at all.

She swore, and clutched the aching wrist in her other hand. "Have to ice this," she murmured. She went into the house, and made herself think of more important things than Colin Foxe.

Vampires, for example.

Vampires were far more important to someone of her ancestry than obsessing over a callous, uncaring, total jerk like Foxe.

Still, whatever his faults, Colin was a human, and she was glad the vampire hadn't hurt him. No human deserved to be attacked by a vampire.

It *had* been a vampire that attacked her, she had no doubt. The pale-haired monster had been a thing of unearthly beauty, looking rather like Legolas gone bad. It had smiled at her, showing long, bright fangs. It had been overwhelmingly male, and utterly repellant.

My species, right or wrong, she thought, going into the kitchen.

She'd known vampires existed all of her life, but she hadn't known if she'd come into contact with them. Her mother's family had been vampire hunters for hundreds of years, and passed the knowledge down from generation to generation. But nobody in the Garrison family had actually hunted vampires for a long time. Nobody had staked a vampire's heart, or cut off its head, since her grandmother's grandparents, she thought. Mia wasn't even sure how accurate anything her grandmother had told her was. She'd read some old records and family diaries, stuff that made the exploits in *Dracula* seem asinine. But the glory days were gone. Apparently there was some kind of truce in effect with the monsters, and most of the hunter families had gotten out of the business of protecting humankind.

But Mia believed the family legends, and the records. She had made a promise to her grandmother on the old woman's deathbed, a promise to prepare herself in case one day the truce was broken. She'd kept herself strong; learned how to defend herself. She'd done everything she could on a physical level, but nobody had taught her *how* to hunt vampires. She'd been hopelessly outclassed in fighting the monster.

She wished she knew how Colin had driven the creature off. She was also thankful that Colin hadn't noticed the monster's otherness. Maybe you needed vampire hunter genes to see them for the monsters they really were.

There was so much she didn't know.

Like how the vampire had found out that there was a hunter, albeit a very untried one, in Los Angeles. However, he'd done it—found her he had. The truce was broken. She had to fight.

She knew that crosses didn't work, but that garlic did. And silver. She'd inherited a silver necklace from her grandmother. It was a wide, flat chain with an intricate locking clasp, which fitted snugly around her neck. It was heavy, hard to fasten with her sore hand, and Mia had never been one for wearing jewelry—but if she didn't want to get bitten in the neck by a vampire, this necklace would probably help.

Probably.

That was the annoying part, knowing what *might* work rather than exactly what *would* work. By tradition, knowledge of vampire hunt-

ing was passed on orally. She had a few docu-
ments to draw on only because somebody in the
last generation of real hunters in the Garrison
family had decided to leave a few obscure,
almost coded clues, just in case.

Sitting alone in her kitchen, pressing an ice
pack to the wrist she'd bruised, and nursing a
broken heart, Mia realized she was woefully
unprepared. And it scared her to death.

It was after dawn when she remembered that
her grandmother had left her a bank safety
deposit box. Maybe there was something hidden
in the box that would help her. All she had to do
now was remember where she'd put the key, and
wait impatiently for the bank to open.

Chapter Three

"Good evening, Lady Serisa." Colin tried not to let his impatience show as he stood at the door of the Matri's Brentwood home. "I need to speak with you."

"And I need to talk to you." The diminutive Matri reached up and tapped him on the forehead with a long, brightly painted fingernail. "Where have you been, boy?"

Being called *boy* didn't suit his Prime's pride. He glared at Serisa, so annoyed that he momentarily forgot the urgency of his mission.

"In case you haven't noticed, we are a telepathic species," she went on tartly. "I may not be *your* Clan Matri, but when I call, you answer."

Colin had been vaguely aware of a nagging voice in the back of his mind, urging him to seek out his own kind, but he hadn't equated it with an actual summons. He hadn't been thinking about vampires lately. He'd been far too occupied with a human woman.

"I have an answering machine," he told Serisa. "And a cell phone and pager on me at all times. You could have called any of my numbers."

"I'm a traditionalist," was her response. "Our secrets are not for sharing in such public ways." She stepped back from the doorway. "Come in."

Colin silently followed the Matri through the house.

The place was large, but in the way of a mansion rather than a Clan Citadel; the tasteful decor showed no evidence that this was the dwelling of a vampire queen. Members of almost all the vampire clans lived in the Los Angeles area, but this was the home territory of the Shagal, led by Matri Serisa and her bondmate, Elder Barak. She was one of the few Matris who chose to live in a crowded human city. His own clan's stronghold was in northern Idaho, which Colin thought was a far more sensible place for the breeding-age females of the Reynards to be hidden away. Though since Serisa was too old to give her clan children, he supposed it didn't matter where she lived.

He really only wanted to give the local Matri his information and leave. He wished he'd called, sent an e-mail, or even used telepathy, when he saw the group gathered in the room where Serisa led him. Apparently he'd interrupted a meeting of the serious, sober, responsible members of the community. Now he was going to have to face all of them.

Boring.

The room was large and windowless, somewhere in the center of the house. There was only one exit, and Serisa lingered in the doorway after she ushered Colin inside. Elder Barak was standing on one side of the room, talking quietly with three other grave elders. They all gave him serious consideration when he stepped into the room.

Colin was relieved to see that Anthony Crowe, from Clan Corvus, was seated in a pale leather chair on the other side of the room. Next to him on a matching couch was Colin's cousin, Alec Reynard, and Alec's bondmate, Domini.

Colin couldn't help but smile at the beautiful, dark-haired female. This drew an automatic frown from Alec, and he put an arm around his bondmate's shoulder.

"Stop it, you two," Domini said, though she leaned into her bondmate's embrace. "Hi, Colin," she added. "You cut your hair."

"You're not supposed to notice details about any Prime but me," Alec said.

Still smiling, Colin sidled closer to this younger group.

"How have you been, kid?" Tony asked. "Haven't seen you around lately."

Colin shrugged. "The team's been busy."

Tony Crowe was retired from the Los Angeles police force. He brightened with interest at Colin's mention of his SWAT team.

"No one is here on a social call," Serisa said, drawing Colin's attention back to her.

"You're usually more fun than this, Aunt Serisa," Tony said. "You could offer the kid a beer."

"I am not pleased with Colin's absence," she answered. "You made a vow," she reminded him. "Remember?"

Her sarcasm stung his pride. "Of course I remember. I can't fulfill a promise if I have nothing to go on."

"How would you know if there was any new information about the Patron if you don't check in with your elders? We haven't had any real contact with you for the last three months."

"That's not true!"

Was it? He'd gone to Arizona to help destroy a lab experimenting on vampires, right after breaking up with Mia. He'd reported on the situation when he got back, then . . .

Colin looked helplessly to Alec. "It hasn't been—"

"Cut the young Prime some slack, Auntie," Alec defended him. "His job fulfills his vow to look after mortals."

"That is not the vow my lady is referring to," Barak spoke up.

"Never mind your work with the police, Colin Foxe," Serisa scolded. "I know what's distracted you. I can feel it whenever I try to touch your thoughts. You've been having sex with a different mortal every night, haven't you?"

"That is what Primes do," Tony pointed out with an unabashed grin.

Mention of mortal women reminded Colin sharply of why he'd come to the Matri. He put aside a sudden rush of dread for Mia and said, "I stopped a Tribe Prime from attacking a human tonight."

Attention focused on him with the intensity of a circle of spotlights, but everyone waited for Serisa to speak.

"Tell me exactly what happened."

At least she hadn't outright dismissed that he'd encountered a Tribe member in her territory. He'd half-expected to be treated like a kid who made up stories.

"This was my fault," Colin began. "That the

mortal was targeted." He'd rehearsed what to say on the way over, but they just kept looking at him, which made it harder to explain coherently. He scratched a sudden itch over his left eyebrow. "I made the mistake of having a long-term relationship with this woman."

"Mistake?" Domini questioned.

"What's *your* definition of long-term?" Tony added. "Two nights?"

"Details, Colin." Serisa's command cut across their sarcasm.

"We were together for three months," Colin answered the Corvus Prime. "Which was long enough for a Tribe bastard to target her for one of their sick games. If I hadn't been in the neighborhood when he attacked her, she'd be wearing his brand by now."

Fury ate at Colin when he thought of how Mia would have been used by the Tribe vampire. But being furious was no way to deliver a report. His police training helped him pull away from personal involvement and see the bigger picture.

"Tribe activity is a threat to mortals and our kind. Fortunately, I was in the neighborhood when the woman was attacked, so we're aware that they're in Clan territory. We can only hope this was the first attack. Now that we know at least one of them is in town, we can concentrate on finding him. Of course, it's likely that he's only one of a pack. I can check out missing persons and assault reports for anomalies that could point to Tribe activity."

"There are psychic ways of tracking," Serisa reminded him.

Colin nodded. "But it doesn't hurt to use every method available to us. The sooner we find him, the safer Mia will be." Colin was appalled at what he'd said, and quickly corrected himself. "The safer all the mortals in the area will be."

"Mia's your girlfriend, right?" Domini asked.

"No," Colin snapped. "We broke up."

"Then why were you with her when this Tribe boy showed up?" Tony asked.

"I told you, it was just a coincidence. I think we need to focus on the fact that a mortal was attacked by a vampire tonight."

"And why aren't you protecting this mortal now, by calling the incident in?" Tony asked.

Tony wasn't on the force now, but he'd been a cop for a very long time, only leaving after decades of service when he couldn't stand wearing facial prosthetics and makeup to make him look older anymore. He might be retired and working as a private investigator, but he still thought and acted like a cop.

Colin didn't want to admit that Mia didn't want his protection. "I plan on heading back there." He looked at Serisa. "Some things you don't phone in."

"You were right to come here," Serisa said. "We will look into the matter." She looked at Alec and Domini. "See that the woman is safe."

The pair of professional bodyguards said, "Yes, Matri."

"Anthony. Find where the Tribe pack is hiding."

Tony stood. "Yes, Matri."

She turned to her longtime bondmate. "Barak will organize a plan of attack."

"Wait a minute!" Colin spoke up. "She's my— You can't— I—"

"You say you are not attached to this woman," Serisa pointed out. "So the threat to her is not your personal concern."

"But—the Tribe's fight was with me. For her."

"You drove him off, but I don't see the woman at your side. You have other work."

The look Serisa gave him assured Colin that no argument was going to change her mind about where his duty lay. And it finally occurred to him that she'd wanted to see him because there was finally a breakthrough in the hunt for the Patron.

He was not at all pleased at the thought of

leaving Mia's welfare in anyone else's hands, but he was Clan Prime. Duty came first. He straightened his shoulders and kept his temper under control. "What do you want me to do, Matri?"

Laurent of the Manticore had one thing that most Tribe vampires didn't possess: a sense of humor. He didn't know where he'd gotten it, or how, but he knew it was damned inconvenient. As a survival tool, it was totally useless.

"I like to think of it as a rather puckish sense of fun," he said to no one in particular as he stood waiting for Justinian's attention to turn his way. He was standing ankle-deep in plush Persian carpet in a windowless bedroom lit only by a few thick red candles. Justinian was currently occupied behind the velvet curtains of the large bed that was the centerpiece of the room. Though there were a half dozen Primes waiting for the pack leader's attention, the only sound was the panting and groaning coming from the girl the king Prime was currently boning. Laurent found the whole situation faintly embarrassing. He also had a hard time refraining from smirking at the melodramatic setting.

That was one of the problems with the Tribes: they took their brand of evil far too seriously. Their sensibilities were anything but postmodern, or even retro camp. It seemed to Laurent that even people who acted like they still lived in the twelfth century ought to acknowledge that they were actually dwelling in the twenty-first. Instead of belonging to the Society for Creative Anachronisms, his dear Tribe *were* anachronisms.

Well, it worked for them. And they were all he had—though he half regretted being called back into the bosom of Tribe Manticore, after so many years on his own.

"Do you find us boring, Laurent?"

Laurent did a good job of hiding his surprise when Justinian suddenly appeared, standing outside the bed curtains. Though he went stiff with an old, familiar fear, he managed to shrug.

"I haven't been back quite long enough to be bored," he answered Justinian. But he didn't meet the pack leader's eyes when he spoke.

The woman in the bed moaned. Laurent was aware of the hunger that stirred among some of the other Primes, but he kept his own urges under control. And his amusement to himself, when Justinian swept a warning gaze across his followers and the testosterone level dropped like a rock.

His feelings weren't hidden from Justinian. "Our Laurent doesn't play pack games." He took a black satin robe from an obsequious mortal servant and tied it on as the mortal quickly bowed his way back into the shadows.

Belisarius, senior among the pack Primes, said, "Laurent doesn't have the balls to hunger for a woman. Not that we'd challenge you," he added with quick deference to Justinian. The other Primes directed derisive laughter at Laurent.

"Do you have balls?" Justinian asked him.

"I do believe I have," Laurent answered. "Now, ask me about what happened tonight, so we can get on with business."

"I take it you didn't bring back the woman."

"He ordered you to do one small thing—" Belisarius began, but Justinian held up a hand to silence him.

"But there were complications."

It wasn't a question. At least Justinian didn't question his competence.

"There was a Clan Prime guarding the woman," Laurent reported. "I thought you'd want to know. I could have just killed him and brought the Garrison woman to you, but that wouldn't get us an explanation about the Clans' involvement with our rightful prey."

"*My* rightful prey," Justinian corrected.

"You should have brought her here," Belisarius said. "To tell us whatever she knows."

"And have the gallant Clan Primes come running to the rescue?" Laurent looked to Justinian. "You told me this was strictly a matter of justified revenge. Is that true?"

"It's not your place to ask questions," Justinian reminded him.

Laurent remembered how he hated that deceptively mild tone, and how dangerous Justinian was when he used it. "Apologies," he said, and bowed his head.

Justinian let a few tense seconds pass before he spoke. "You were correct not to bring the mortal here. Watch her, Laurent. We'll let her think she's free, while we discover her connection to the Clans."

Chapter Four

Three days later

"Would you like another iced tea?"

Mia looked away from the airplane window at the flight attendant's question. "No, thank you. How soon until we land?"

"About half an hour," the woman answered.

She smiled hopefully, but when Mia didn't request anything else, she moved to the back of the plane. Mia was the only passenger on the small jet flying back to Los Angeles from Colorado, and she wasn't making much work for the staff on her great-grandfather's jet.

The fact that her great-grandfather had a private airplane, and that he'd put it at her disposal, was still pretty shocking. Yes, she'd known he was very rich, but being exposed to the rarefied atmosphere where the super wealthy dwelled made her breathless.

She'd expected the telephone number her grandmother had left her would put her in immediate contact with her great-grandfather, but it hadn't worked out that way. The number belonged to a law firm. She'd used the code phrase that went along with the number, which got a very complicated ball rolling.

Getting to see her elderly relative face to face had taken her through several layers of flunkies; men in more and more expensive offices and suits; men with blanker and blanker faces and blander voices.

Finally, a rough old voice on a speaker phone in the fanciest office of all had ordered the expensive lawyer out.

When she was alone, the old man said, "What do you want?"

It turned out to be very hard to say the words. What if she was making a complete fool of herself? What if it was all myth after all? What if what had attacked her hadn't been—what she thought? What if this wasn't actually Henry Garrison?

But she took a deep breath and said, "I want to know how to hunt vampires."

"Why?" was the gruff reply.

"Somebody has to," was the only answer she could think of.

"For the sake of family tradition? Or is it more personal?"

She thought for a moment before she said, "Both, I guess. I was attacked by a vampire, and I—"

"You've had actual contact with one? Did it take your blood?"

"Yes. No. I—"

"Do you know where it is?"

"Somewhere in Los Angeles."

"That's a lot of territory to cover."

"I know. That's why I need your help. I'm willing to hunt it, but I need to know how."

A soft cackle of laughter issued from the speaker. Then the old man was silent for a while. "All right," he said at last. "I'll show you."

After that she'd been whisked off in a succession of limousines and airplanes, and finally into an SUV that took her up a mountain road to a mansion in the center of a walled compound. Once inside this luxurious fortress, she'd finally come face to face with the last vampire hunter in the family.

Her great-grandfather was not a rush-up-and-give-him-a-big-hug-and-call-him-Grandpa kind of person, but Mia hadn't expected him to be. What she hadn't expected him to be was—kind of creepy. The time she'd spent with him had been instructive, but it hadn't been particularly pleasant. In fact, he spent more time hunched over a laptop working on financial dealings than actually looking at her when they were together. The man was cold, abrupt, and there was a—hunger—in him for vampires.

The fact that he wanted her to bring him a live one freaked her at first.

But his explanation made sense. He reminded her that vampire hunting was almost a dead art. Times had changed, and it would be intelligent to find out what sorts of modern weaponry worked on the monsters.

When he first brought the subject up, Mia was outraged at the idea of experimenting on a living creature. But her great-grandfather pointed out that that was exactly what vampires were—creatures, monsters, parasites.

The Enemy.

She'd signed on to fight a war. There couldn't be any room for mercy when fighting the forces of evil.

That sounds so melodramatic.

Yet it was true. And she had promised to capture a vampire and bring it to her great-grandfather. He'd provided her with drugs that he promised rendered the monsters helpless.

She'd figure out something. And she'd have to do it alone. Even with her new knowledge, Mia still felt unprepared for the challenge.

Oh, no, you don't, Caramia Luchese. I am as tough as nails, and I can do this.

Only it would be so much better if she didn't have to do it by herself. Her great-grandfather had promised her help in transporting the vampire once she'd caught it, but insisted that the capture was her duty alone.

She didn't get it.

Maybe it was some sort of hunter tradition of going mano a mano against the forces of evil. Though if that was the way it was done, it was no wonder the hunter families had died out or gotten out of the business.

Maybe it was a test.

Maybe if she brought her great-grandfather the vampire, he would provide her with more information and resources. Well, she needed his help, so she'd do it his way for now.

She just wished she could tell someone. Unreasonably, stupidly, the one person she wanted to tell was Colin Foxe.

I can't trust him on an emotional level—but damn, the man can kick ass.

Damn, but the man also *had* a fine ass.

Mia ran a hand through her short curls and

wondered where that thought had come from. Probably because he'd shown up the other night and—she hated to admit it—saved *her* ass. She'd had a primal reaction to it then that she'd managed to cover with anger, but the effects still lingered. Only pride had kept her from dragging him down on the ground and giving herself to him. She'd felt his excitement after the fight, knew the cockiness he got from the victory. The sex would have been hard, fast, and sweet.

She closed her eyes and tasted the man's kisses, felt his hands on her. The memories alone were enough to stir instant, aching heat.

She had good reasons to hate the man, but he made a hell of a sex toy.

Which was another reason not to bring him into this. She couldn't afford emotional involvement—not lust, not hate. It wouldn't be good for her edge, or his. Besides, how could she get him to believe in vampires? He'd scoff until one was sucking the life out of him.

This thought brought up lovely images of her rescuing him, his gratitude, and her cheerfully rebuffing the gorgeous bastard.

"We'll be landing in a few moments."

The flight attendant's voice brought Mia out of her reverie. This is not a game, she reminded herself as she checked to make sure her seatbelt was fastened.

"What do you mean, you can't guard her if you can't find her?" Colin demanded of his cousin over the cellular phone. "Why can't you find her?" Why had he left Mia's welfare to anyone else?

He stepped out of the small office building of the Van Trier Executive Airport with his phone pressed to his ear, and sudden anger bursting inside him. Even though the sun was setting, he automatically put on sunglasses. His gaze was drawn across the parking lot toward a small jet making a landing on one of the airport's two runways. He put a finger in his left ear to block out the engine noise.

Alec Reynard's voice sounded far too cheerful when he answered. "The best we can figure is that your girlfriend left home voluntarily."

"She's not my girlfriend. And how do you figure that?" Colin shouted over the roar of airport noise.

"Domini and I broke into her house. There was no scent or sign of any vampire having been in the place but you. There was a string of garlic on the back door, so maybe she suspects vampires exist."

"She's Italian," Colin answered, "and she likes to cook. The back door's in the kitchen."

"That's what Domini suggested. You've spent a lot of time over there, have you?"

"You don't believe the girl's in danger, do you?"

"I haven't found any evidence of her being involved with our kind, except for you calling me every hour."

This was only the second time Colin had enquired about Mia, as he hadn't had the time, but he let it go. He didn't know why Alec was needling him and not taking the situation seriously. "Has Tony found—"

"He found and lost the trail of the one you fought, but no evidence of a pack operating in the area yet. Let's hope it was a lone Prime passing through who decided to have a little fun with you."

It would be a relief to think that the Tribe was long out of town. "Tony's still checking, though, right?"

"Of course. And how's your assignment coming along?"

"Slowly," Colin answered. "My team spent most of the last few days on that bank robbery situation that was all over the news. Then we had to do a debrief, and a training sim to see how we could handle it better."

The rest of his team had gone home wrung out and ragged. Colin wasn't tired the way his mortal teammates were, but he was glad for the days off they'd been given. For some reason, he'd found that he was slightly envious of the wives and families the rest of the team had to go home to.

"Now I finally have some time off to work on the Patron info I'm supposed to check out."

"And?" Alec prompted.

"I'm at the airport now. I persuaded a beautiful young woman to look through all the confidential client files, but it's going to take her a while."

"Do you think you've finally run down a lead on this Patron?"

Impatience clawed at Colin. When he'd helped shut down the Patron's immortality research facility in Arizona, he and the others had made their escape on a stolen Gulfstream jet. Tracing the ownership information of the airplane should have quickly led to the identity of the Patron.

Instead it had led to plowing slowly through layers and layers of financial camouflage. The man hid his identity well. After all this time, they still didn't know who the plane belonged to, but some maintenance records had finally been tracked down. That paper trail led to this small, private airport. Now all Colin could do was wait while the mortal female he'd flirted with and hypnotized into helping him looked through confidential files.

He tried to put his mind on how good-looking the office worker was, to stop thinking about Mia, but heard himself say, "Why couldn't the woman stay home so she can be protected?"

"Maybe the woman thinks she can take care of herself," Reynard said.

Colin had forgotten that he was on the phone. "Mortals need taking care of, especially females."

The wave of awareness hit him even before he stopped speaking. If Reynard answered, Colin didn't hear him. All he was aware of was Mia stepping off the plane that had just landed. He was waiting by the gate by the time she reached it. Her gaze was on the ground, a frown of concentration on her face.

"What are you doing here?" he asked.

Her head jerked up, and their gazes met. For a moment there was a light of welcome in her eyes that took Colin's breath away. He almost took her in his arms, but her expression changed to guarded suspicion that warned him to keep his distance.

"What are *you* doing here?" she questioned him.

"Business," was his answer. He moved to let

her through the gate and kept pace with her as she walked across the parking lot. "Where have you been?"

"Out of town."

"I know. Why?"

She stopped, and glared at him. "How did you know? Why do you want to know?"

"You were attacked. I wanted to make sure you were safe."

"So you tracked me down here?"

"No. I told you I'm on business."

She took a deep breath, and Colin felt her pull her emotions in and get herself under control. "Thank you for your concern, Officer Foxe."

If she could attempt to be reasonable, so could he. He put his hand on her arm. He was aware of the muscles beneath the warm softness of her skin. That was Mia, steel and velvet. She trembled ever so slightly at his touch, wanting him, and fighting that wanting. He felt the same way. The need was always instant between them.

"Come on, let me drive you home."

She didn't answer, but she did let him lead her toward his car.

But as they passed the small airport office, the office manager stepped out of the doorway. "Officer Foxe!" she called, and hurried up to him.

Standing too close to him, she tilted her head provocatively and said, "I found those records you asked for." She smiled, and the look she gave him was both pleased and hopeful.

Mia stiffened, emotions going cold as ice, and stepped away from Colin. "I have a ride."

Colin moved toward Mia, but the other woman put herself between them. She touched his shoulder. "Come into my office, and I'll show you what I've found."

Damn! Damn! Damn! The woman was beautiful, and he had come on to her. But he hadn't expected Mia to be here!

Now Mia was walking away, and she was likely reminding herself that he'd broken up with her because he'd told her he wasn't interested in being involved with only one woman. Which was the truth, but he still felt as if he'd somehow been caught cheating on her.

Which didn't change the fact that he did need the information the woman had found for him. He'd stop by Mia's place later to check on her.

"Good work," he said, turning a smile on the waiting woman. He put his arm around her slender shoulders, turning her back toward the building. "Let's have a look at what you've found."

Chapter Five

Laurent slept with women. He drank their blood. He took their money. It was a good life. And most important, this low-key lifestyle let him live in choice territory claimed by the Clans without them being any the wiser. He'd been dwelling safely and happily in the warm California nights until his sire showed up with a pack of Primes and all their emotional baggage, and demanded Laurent do his bidding.

He wished he hadn't been lured back into the machinations of Tribe Manticore.

Being an exile had its advantages.

Besides, he only might be my sire. It's not likely he'll say so one way or the other. He uses the truth to keep me in line. If I'm a good little slave, someday he might tell me. Typical tribal behavior.

"But I'm only really in it for the money."

Justinian had said something about their finding out what the Clans knew about Laurent's quarry, but Laurent hadn't heard any news after two nights of hunting. And this was after he'd gone to the trouble of providing the pack with cell phones and teaching them how to use them—after convincing Justinian that this modern method of communicating was safer around Clan boys than using telepathy, since mental activity was more likely to be looked for.

He snorted, and concentrated on the area below his roof perch, where he had a clear view of the entrance of the building across the street. Tonight would be the night.

This was the third night he'd staked out the fitness center where the Garrison woman worked out. This had seemed a safer place to wait for her than her house, where the Clan Prime might be lurking—waiting for Laurent. She was an exercise fanatic, and bound to show up sometime.

"And there she is," he murmured as he spotted the dark-haired young mortal turn the corner and come striding toward the glass doors of the gym. Energy, purpose, and righteous anger crackled through her aura like flashes of lightning.

It was too bad she was Justinian's prey, because Laurent would quite enjoy a taste of this gifted mortal woman. He shrugged. Maybe after the pack leader was done with her—not that she'd have much spirit left then.

He let himself fantasize while she went into the building. When she left the gym, he could follow her back to her car and take her there. It was a simple, neat plan.

And foiled within a few seconds when the Clan vampire he'd fought for her came walking around the same corner, and followed the woman into the fitness center.

Laurent drew all his mental shielding tightly around himself and kept his swearing silent and on the surface of his mind.

Why couldn't this go easily?

He sighed. After he was sure the Clan vampire had no awareness of him, Laurent took out his cellular telephone.

Maybe, just maybe, he could get someone in the Manticore pack to answer, and give him a little backup.

"Oh, for crying out loud, what are you doing here?" Mia demanded when Colin Foxe walked into the martial arts room.

Bare-chested, he wore a pair of loose-fitting gray sweatpants. There was no one else in this small area but the two of them, so she couldn't just ignore him in the crowd.

He smiled in that infuriatingly charming way of his, and his sultry dark eyes glinted beneath the heavy arch of his brows. "I have a membership."

"But you haven't been here since we broke up."

His smile widened. "You've noticed."

Mia was tempted to keep her claws out and continue snarling at the man, but what good would it do? It would only let him know that she still hurt. It wasn't likely that he was here to explain about the bimbo at the airport, or to apologize for his continuing existence. He certainly wasn't here to beg her to take him back. She knew she should wrap herself in pride and dignity and simply ignore his presence, but curiosity got the better of her.

"You followed me here, didn't you?"

"Yes."

"Because you're feeling protective, Officer Foxe?"

"Yep."

While she rather admired this trait in him, she wished he was feeling protective toward somebody else. "It was a random act of violence that you came upon by accident. Having done the Good Samaritan thing, you can go back to forgetting about me now."

"I take 'serve and protect' seriously."

"Which is about all you take seriously." Damn! There she went being bitter and sarcastic again. "Never mind my whining," she added. "It's late. I'm tired. I want to get in a workout and go home."

She'd wanted to go to bed the minute she got home, but a hunter needed to be disciplined. She hadn't expected Colin to be part of her workout regime.

Colin looked around the empty room and gestured her toward a mat. "Come on. Try to beat me up. You'll feel better."

"I don't want to *try*."

He laughed. "I know." His gaze flicked over her, all hot and arrogant. "You are so sexy when you're pissed off."

It was such a blatant come-on that Mia laughed. After three months of callous abandonment, he thought that she still couldn't resist him.

"You are so—"

"A pig. I know." He spun around and did a backflip onto the sparring mat. He was lithe, lean, wiry as Jet Li.

"I'm impressed," she told him.

Mia crossed to a punching bag set up on a heavy floor stand and proceeded to take out her aggression with some kickboxing moves. She could feel him watching her, which made her clumsy. Which did nothing for her temper. She was *used* to practicing with a group. She'd been doing this for ye—

"You don't look like you've been doing this for years."

She turned in puzzlement at Colin's sarcastic comment. He was closer than she thought, and he lunged toward her. Though she was off balance, Mia reacted to defend herself.

For the next few minutes they punched, blocked, feinted, and kicked their way around the practice room. There was nothing formal about what they did; it was the closest thing to street fighting Mia'd ever experienced.

It was intense, exciting, punctuated by adrenaline and rising lust.

Becoming aware of where this dance was leading, Mia came to a stop. She put up her hands, and Colin backed away. He looked bright and fresh, like he could go on like this all night. She was sweaty and breathing hard.

"You did good," he told her. He bounced on the balls of his feet, grinning. "More?"

It was tempting to continue going at it with Colin, but she knew that come-and-get-me look in his eyes was also an I'm-gonna-have-you promise. And she wanted him, just like she always wanted him, especially at times like this when his hands had been on her, and hers on him.

She wanted at the same time to hurt him and to fall on the mat with him and go at it like bunnies.

So for his safety, and her self-respect, Mia said, "No."

He tilted his head to one side, and looked up from under dark, thick eyelashes. "You sure?"

Now he was being cute. She didn't need that. She picked up a towel and wiped off her face. "I need a shower. And don't take that as an invitation to join me."

"Is sex all you think about?"

She couldn't help but laugh. "That's my line."

He gave a slight shrug. "You know how I like variety. And I've never done it in the girl's locker room."

Mia didn't say anything else, and when she left the workout room, he didn't follow her, yet she could feel his attention focused tightly on her. She was aware of his straining not to come after her, and she knew he was aware of her fight to keep from going back to him. It was a victory that she made it out to the hall and down the stairs.

She hoped he wouldn't be waiting for her after she took a long, hot shower and then lingered in the locker room for a long talk with a friend. But Colin was waiting by the entrance when she came upstairs, his back to her. He was facing the wide glass doors, talking on his cell phone. There was no way out of the building but past him.

She heard him say, "Thanks, Dom." Then he turned around, smiling at her, the phone already off and tucked away.

She didn't know what to make of this man who had left her suddenly getting so clingy. "I'm fine," she insisted, waving him toward the door. "Go home."

"Right," he said, taking her by the arm. "Let's go home. I'll drive."

"My car's in the lot."

"I know. Mine's parked next to it. I'll drive."

"Oh, for crying out—"

"What were you doing at the airport?" he asked as he ushered her outside.

The fitness center was open twenty-four/seven, and it was late. There was little traffic on the street, and no one on the sidewalk but the two of them. This privacy, and the intimacy of his hand on her arm, disturbed Mia greatly. It depressed her, as well. Even his solicitousness was depressing.

It seemed like Colin was always taking her home. To *her* home, never his. She really knew very little about him, except that he loved being the knight in shining Kevlar, and was great in bed. And that he *couldn't be tied down by one woman.*

"If I answer your question, will you answer one for me, for once?"

"I told you I was on business," he anticipated her question. "That woman didn't mean anything to me."

Mia chuckled. "What you do with other women is not my business," she reminded him.

"You were jealous."

"I was annoyed at myself."

"For being jealous."

"What is the matter with you?" she demanded. "I'm trying to be civil, but you keep—coming on to me."

"Sorry," he said, and let go of her. "Is that better?"

She nodded, though she could still feel the possessive warmth of his touch on her skin.

"Now, where have you been? What were you doing at the airport?"

She didn't know why he sounded suspicious. Maybe just because he was a cop.

"I was out of town doing research." It was more or less the truth; let Colin think it was research for a story. "And caught a ride home on a private plane. My turn?"

They turned the corner and walked uphill toward the three-story parking garage at the end of the block. An alley cut between the fitness center building and the garage. The streetlights were spaced farther apart on this side street, and the one nearest the parking lot was out. There was suddenly something very still and spooky about the darkness.

Fighting off primitive uneasiness, Mia said, "I heard about a bank robbery that SWAT was called in on, while I was in the locker room."

Her friend had said, "The news said that a sharpshooter took out two of the robbers. Was that your boyfriend?"

"Were you the shooter?" Mia asked Colin. She felt him tense.

"It was me."

She stopped and turned to face him, putting a hand on his arm. "Are you okay?"

He nodded.

Colin stared at the mortal woman. Just when he thought she was going to rag on him some more about their breakup, she started worrying about him. Every time he convinced himself that his fascination with her was purely sexual, she did something that rattled him.

"I'm fine," he told her, too aware of her touch, too aware of her compassion. "I'm bloodthirsty, remember?" There was no way a mortal woman could understand and accept this literal truth the way a vampire female would.

"Good," she said, growing suddenly tense. She looked around very slowly and carefully, and whispered, "I think bloodthirsty is about to come in handy."

He became aware of the threat a moment before she spoke.

Mia no doubt saw shadows moving toward them, two out of the alley up ahead, and another pair from around the corner behind them.

What he noticed before seeing any shapes was dark mental energy, the malevolent psychic signature of Tribe vampires. They'd dropped their shielding as one, wanting him to know they were there. The intensity of their regard sent a stab of pain through his head.

"Games," he said, and smiled grimly. His blood suddenly sang with the joy of the hunt. "I like games."

"Colin, I think—"

"Don't think. Go on instinct."

She took something out of her gym bag. If it was a gun it wasn't going to do any good, but he didn't tell her so.

"Parking lot," he said. Grabbing her around the waist, he picked her up and ran.

Chapter Six

Mia might have protested being carried like a child, if she wasn't so shocked at Colin's speed and agility. It seemed like it only took him a few steps to reach and dart around the two vampires in the alley. She caught the flash of fangs and glowing eyes as they passed, and brought her hand up enough to squeeze off a blast of aerosol into the vampire's face.

When his only reaction was a sputtered cough and a slight turning of his head, she realized she'd pulled out a canister of pepper spray instead of the garlic mixture she'd reached for. But at least it took the monster's attention away from Colin for a moment.

As Colin sprinted ahead, she could hear the footsteps of the two from the street pounding up to join the ones from the alley.

Somebody yelled, "This is no way to run an ambush. I told you to wait!"

"You don't give orders, exile," an arrogant voice answered.

While the vampires behind them argued, Colin leaped over a ramp barrier and put her down on the other side. All the parking stalls on the ground floor were empty. Her breathing seemed to echo loudly in the vacant space. The garage wasn't well lit, and Colin dragged her farther into shadow behind a thick concrete pillar.

"Don't worry," he told her. "I've called for backup."

She had no idea when he could possibly have done that, but this was hardly the time to argue. "Those—men—" She tried to warn him, but she didn't know how. "Did you see their—"

"Great makeup. It's a cult. Don't worry about it."

He was right, there was no time to worry. "How do we get out of here?"

"Up," he said. He snatched her gym bag from her and dropped it on the ground. "Run," he ordered, and gave her a slight push.

Mia pelted up the curve of the parking ramp. The sooner she got to her car, the sooner she could get to the antivampire weapons stowed in the trunk.

She was aware of the pounding of her feet on the concrete, of the roar of her heart and her own breathing, but she didn't hear Colin behind her. Even a quick look back would slow her down, though, and she needed those weapons!

Besides, Colin was a dangerous man, and he could move silent as a cat.

She didn't look back even when she heard shouts, or the meaty sound of a blow. A few more steps, and she'd reached the second level, where her car was parked.

Damn it! Her keys were in the bag Colin had tossed aside.

She started to turn back, then felt air coldly caress her face as something flew past. The next moment, a vampire was standing in front of her. It was the pale-haired one who'd first come after her.

Mia came to a jarring halt, just in time to keep from running into the monster's widespread arms.

"We meet again," he said.

He was smug, smiling, and even in the semi-darkness she could see the obscenely long fangs protruding over his red lips. He held out a taloned hand.

"Come along, and nobody gets hurt," he told her.

"He's lying!" Colin shouted from below. "Don't let him touch you!"

"Don't listen to him," the vampire said. "You'll beg for my protection after he's dead."

She heard the sounds of fighting. Colin was outnumbered, surrounded. He needed help.

The vampire stepped toward her, and she backpedaled quickly. Her impulse was to turn and run, but Mia couldn't bear to turn her back on the fanged creature.

"Enough of this," he said, and rushed toward her.

Mia dove sideways and flattened herself on the concrete.

A vehicle swerved into the parking lot below, crashing through the barrier, and then its bright headlights raked up the curving ramp ahead of the roaring engine. Mia watched in astonishment as two figures jumped out the back doors while the huge SUV was still moving. And suddenly Colin wasn't alone in fighting the vampires.

The car kept coming, as big as a tank, straight toward the blond vampire. He jumped just an instant before the SUV would have hit him, landed on the roof with a heavy thud of boots, then leaped again completely into thin air from the second story of the garage.

As he disappeared, the SUV came to a halt next to where Mia cowered against the ramp's inside wall. The driver opened the door and looked calmly down at Mia.

"Hi, I'm Domini. The guy with the beard down there is Tony. The one with the cleft chin is my Alec." The dark-haired woman got out and helped Mia to her feet. "Welcome to—" She put her arm out to stop Mia from running toward the fighting.

"Colin needs help!" Mia protested.

"Help's here," Domini said. "No need for us to interrupt the boys when they're fighting. You know how much they enjoy it."

The woman's cheerfulness and enigmatic words confused Mia further. "Who are you? What are you doing here? And thanks," she added, finally realizing that she'd been rescued from the vampires. Relief flooded her as she realized who the rescuers might be. "Are you hunt—"

Colin ran up to her before she could finish. The next thing she knew, she was wrapped in his tight embrace, and his mouth came down hard and fiercely on hers. All the fear and excitement in her shifted instantly to desire, and she responded just as hungrily. She lost herself to the need.

Until someone coughed loudly.

Domini said, "You guys want to use the back seat? Concrete can be so hard on the back."

"And the knees," one of the men added.

Someone else said, "There are alarms going off. We really ought to leave before the police—"

"The police are here," Colin said, lifting his head from hers.

"But this isn't the kind of rumble you want to report," one of the men said.

Mia was glad that Colin's arms were around her, because her knees were weak. She supposed she ought to be embarrassed by this visceral reaction to danger, but it felt so right to be alive and with Colin. Her body was full of lust, but she fought to focus her attention on the three newcomers. Domini, Tony, and Alec were all tall, dark-haired, attractive, and dressed in black.

"What happened to the—those—" While everyone stared at her, Mia finally remembered what Colin had called their attackers. "Cultists?" She couldn't bring herself to use the word *vampire* until she was sure of who their rescuers were. "Who are you?" she added.

"The cowards ran away when my backup showed." Colin gestured toward the one with the chin. "That's my cousin Alec, and his lady Domini. And that's her cousin—"

"Identifications have already been made," Domini interrupted him.

Tony gave her a charming smile. "You're Mia. I'm delighted. Let's go," he said to Colin.

Colin glared at Tony. "I thought you said there weren't any of them in town."

"I said I hadn't found any yet. Looks like they found you."

"Why?" Alec questioned.

"Has anyone asked the local hunters if they know anything?" Domini questioned. "Aren't they the ones who keep tabs on the bad guys?"

Tony made a sour face. "We don't communicate much with—them."

"Maybe we should. Look, I could—"

"No," Tony cut her off. "I said I'd find out about their being in town. I'll set up a meeting with the hunters—cranks and loons though they are."

The man didn't sound at all happy about it, but Mia was overjoyed to hear mention of local hunters. Chances were that Colin and his friends thought that vampires were some kind of nut cult. Tony clearly thought that those who hunted so-called vampires were also nuts, so this was no time to point out that vampires were real, and that she was a hunter.

Still, if this Tony could help her contact the local hunters . . .

"Come on," Colin said. He led her up the ramp. "Now I really am going to drive you home."

Chapter Seven

The only thing that seemed real in the whole surrealistic incident was Colin's kissing her. Mia's lips were still alive with the memory of it, and her body sparked with need.

But information was more important than need. Her world had changed so radically in the last few days, she didn't know what reality was anymore. Now it looked like even Colin had secrets connected with the dark underworld she'd so recently entered. She needed to know them without giving her own away.

"Colin, I—"

"Don't ask," he said.

Mia's hand was on his arm. He didn't think she was aware of touching him, but the contact sizzled all through him. She'd sat beside him on the drive, stunned and confused, and the hunger for each other buzzed silently between them.

Now as he turned onto her street, she was growing curious, restless, wanting answers.

"Those people," she said. "Your relatives. What were they doing—"

"I shouldn't have introduced you."

What was wrong with him? How stupid was he? By all that was holy and sane in his world, he had no business giving information and the names of his kind to an outsider, a mortal.

"I told you I called for backup," he told her. "One of them is a retired cop. The other two—"

Damn! He was doing it again. When had it gotten so easy to spill his guts to this woman who was supposed to be a passing fancy?

"Forget about them," he said. "Your knowing about them isn't important. You won't see them again."

"Why not?" Mia asked. Her attitude stiffened with hurt and anger. "Aren't I good enough to meet your family?"

The question, and the pain she tried to hide, tore Colin in two opposite directions. He couldn't very well say, "No, not really," without hurting her further. He hadn't meant to drag her into his world, a place where she did not belong.

"What were they doing there?" she asked. "What do they—you—have to do with this so-called vampire cult?"

"I can't answer that."

He was going to have to make her forget it all, especially any reference to vampires. But the woman was both stubborn and psychic. It wasn't going to be easy to alter her memories.

"Won't answer, you mean."

"Yeah. Won't," he admitted. "I'm sorry you've gotten involved." He pulled into her driveway and turned off the engine.

He could tell his words weren't reassuring her. In fact, he felt her growing not only annoyed, but more suspicious by the moment.

"Why have you really been following me?" she demanded. "Why are you always around lately? I know you don't want anything to do with me, so there's an ulterior motive, isn't there? Are you using me as bait to draw these— cultists—out?"

"That's a good theory," he admitted. "But the farthest thing from the truth. All I want to do is help you."

Maybe he *had* sort of been stalking her, but he'd thought the only harm was to his own sanity. The results were proving dangerously unhealthy for her, though, as well as for his mental health.

"This is all my fault, Mia. I can't explain, and I know you don't think you have any reason to trust me. And you don't, not on a personal level.

But I will get these nuts out of your life, and keep you safe. Then I'll go."

"Maybe I don't—"

Another car pulled in behind his. Was she going to tell him she didn't want him to stay, or that she didn't want him to go? He got out of his car and hurried toward the other vehicle.

Tony Crowe stepped out of Mia's car and tossed her gym bag and keys to Colin. "Thought the lady would like to have these."

Colin caught Mia's stuff and glanced behind him. Mia was standing in the driveway. It was his turn to toss the keys to her as she started toward them. "Go inside."

"I beg your—"

Go inside.

The telepathic order came not only from him but from Tony, as well. Though Tony did add *please* when he intruded into Mia's mind.

Go to bed, Colin said. *Sleep.*

Mia moved with slow reluctance, and kept glancing back toward them as she went toward the front door.

Colin glared at the other Prime when she was safely inside the house. "I don't need your help."

"Yeah. You do," Tony declared bluntly. "Remember Serisa's plan for this mortal? You aren't part of it. Alec, Domini, and I are supposed to protect the woman and find the Tribe pack. Your job is to take out the Patron. What were you doing with her tonight?"

"Protecting her," Colin answered. "Which was more than you were doing. I knew where to find her—"

"Which you should have told one of us."

"I want to protect her."

"Does she belong to you, then? Do you claim her?"

"Of course not!"

"Then do as you're told."

"Serisa of Shagal is not my Matri. She can make suggestions, but she does not rule me. I am Prime."

Tony shook his head. "Don't ask for trouble, kid. This mortal woman dwells in Shagal territory. By right, Serisa of Shagal has jurisdiction over how all mortals in her territory are protected. Now, if you claim Mia Luchese and bring her into our world—"

"Don't be ridiculous."

"What's ridiculous about it? Mortal women are brought into the Clans all the time. If you want, I—"

Possessive fury warred with outrage, and the world went red around him. Colin lashed out at Tony without thinking.

The other Prime backed away before the blow could touch him and held his hands out in front of him. "Whoa! Calm down. This isn't the time or place for a couple of Primes to get into it."

"Are you challenging me?" Colin demanded. "For *her*?" Jealousy pounded through him, and he didn't care where or when, or with who he got into a fight with over Mia. "First the Tribe, and now you. What's so fascinating about my female, that everybody wants her?"

"I thought you didn't want her."

"I want her until I say otherwise," Colin declared.

"Kid, you are not making a bit of sense."

The worst part was, Colin knew he wasn't. And it was all because of Mia. Not that it was her fault, but . . .

"I am not a kid," he reminded Tony. "I am Prime."

"Yeah, yeah. You've been out of the nest for what, five, six years? Sometimes when Primes get the bonding call early, they go a little nuts."

"Bonding?" Cold fear ran up Colin's spine. "What the hell are you talking about?" he shouted at the older Prime.

"Are you trying to wake up the whole neighborhood?"

The sharp question from Tony brought Colin

back to his senses. But before he could deny the accusation of bonding, the door opened and Mia stepped out of the house.

"What's going on?" she asked as she came toward them.

She'd changed into a short silk nightgown. All Colin was aware of for a moment was the outline of her body beneath the clinging fabric, and the length of her shapely legs. Looking at her drove him crazy.

"Hello, there," Tony said.

Colin swore under his breath. Then he said to the other vampire, "I'll deal with her. Get out of here."

Tony looked concerned as he glanced between Colin and the mortal, but he didn't argue. He shrugged, smiled, and disappeared into the night.

That only left Mia to deal with, and Colin wasn't quite sure what to do. His arms came around her automatically when she reached him, and she leaned her warm, curving body into his embrace. His mouth came hungrily down on hers without any conscious volition, and she responded with equal need. He picked her up and carried her into the house, and she was the one who slammed the door with her foot once they were inside.

Chapter Eight

$\mathscr{M}$ia didn't fully understand what was happening when Colin brought her into the living room and they tumbled to the floor together. She'd thought she'd been dreaming about the men arguing in the driveway. It was as if she'd obeyed a hypnotic command to sleep, but hadn't really. It was all very confusing. But apparently she'd been outside in her nightgown, where Colin had been arguing with Tony . . .

And she didn't care, because Colin's touch set her on fire. This was the craziest night of her life. Everything was too intense, too weird.

And being caressed by Colin was too wonderful for her to say, *What the hell do you think you're doing?* Or *Get out of my house!*

She could barely think those things, and he'd know she didn't mean them anyway.

All they needed right now was to be together, thoughts and bodies entwined, melted into one.

It had been like that from the moment they met—as though he could read her mind, and sometimes she could read his. It often became impossible to tell who was touching who, who was satisfying who. They simply disappeared into each other.

In the last three months she'd mourned that intimate connection as much as she'd missed the frantic, fierce, totally consuming way she and Colin made love.

Never mind that he'd left her. Never mind that he would leave her again. She *needed* what he was doing right now. And she wanted him in her bedroom. Pride should keep her from reacting like this.

All she could do was gasp and arch her back when he brought her gown up and over her head. The silk moved against her skin with a sensual slither, drawing sparks of need along her nerves.

He cupped her breasts, teased her hard nipples, then brushed his fingers over her belly and between her thighs. The touch was soft, feathery, and swift, almost all over her at once. Sensation rippled through her, making her frantic.

What good was pride, when she'd never wanted him to leave her bed in the first place?

With a twist and a firm push, Mia put Colin on his back on the hardwood floor. He made a sound between a growl and a laugh, and she echoed it as she pulled off his T-shirt and tugged down his trousers to get at his hot, hard-muscled flesh.

There was nothing gentle in the way she caressed him, or the hungry way her mouth moved over him, nipping as much as kissing his chest and shoulders and throat. God, how she'd missed the taste and scent and texture of him! She wanted to eat him up!

"Draw blood if you want to," he growled as her teeth skimmed his jaw and throat. "Cause I'm going to."

His hands smoothed up her back and down her sides to cup her ass. Then he flipped her onto her back, and was buried inside her in one hard thrust.

Mia arched up to meet the force of his entry and the swift, plunging strokes that filled her again and again. She loved it this way—fast, frantic, reckless, consuming. She closed her eyes, riding the shattering waves of pleasure.

Then there was a moment of sharp pain, and Mia was lost to the ecstasy.

She was a feast, and he'd been starving too long. Colin buried himself in her soft heat while his fangs pierced the tender flesh of her breast. He suckled there even after he collapsed on top of her, his body spent and sated. Even beyond the sex, the taste of her filled his senses with more intensity than ever. Possessing every part of her was like nothing else in the world.

Damn, he'd missed her! How did she do this to him? Why was Mia so perfect? Her spirit was the perfect challenge. Her body gave him perfect sex. Her blood brought him the perfect high.

Colin was almost grateful to the vampires for attacking her, or he wouldn't be here with her now.

When the memory of the attack intruded on his feeding, he lifted his head, abruptly denying himself the fiery taste he craved. As delicious as Mia's essence was, he had a more important reason for taking her blood than the sheer pleasure of it. Selfish he might be, but there was a higher purpose at work here.

Colin rolled to his side, took a deep breath, and forced his eyes to clear from red-tinged night sight, to focus with more human vision on the woman lying beside him. She drifted somewhere between sleep and waking, her body satisfied and utterly relaxed. It wasn't possible to keep from touching her, so he brushed his fingers across her cheeks and through her dark hair. He relished the way the short curls twined around his fingers, but it also reminded him that he couldn't afford having a human woman clinging to him.

Right now she needed his protection. Though he supposed a proper Prime would not have used protecting a woman he'd left as an excuse to have sex with her.

"Tough," he murmured, unable to call up much guilt for what he'd just done.

Should he make a promise to a matri that it wouldn't happen again? He wasn't that strong, or unselfish. And why shouldn't the humans sometimes pay just a little for the protection Primes gave them? Especially when the payment gave the human as much pleasure as it did the Prime.

Colin smiled, in no doubt about what Mia had gotten from the exchange. He'd been exquisitely aware of all her responses, reveled in all the orgasms he'd given her.

He bent down and kissed her throat. Lust coursed through him, but he was caught in an even deeper wave of pure affection.

He got to his feet with her in his arms, naked and blissed out, and carried her upstairs to the bedroom, where he could conduct the delicate mental work of convincing her mind that almost everything that had happened tonight hadn't been at all what it seemed.

He had even less guilt about brainwashing Mia than he had about the sex.

Mia woke with a faint taste of copper in her mouth; an odd but not unpleasant sensation. There was also a ringing in her ears, and it took her a muzzy moment to realize that the sound was her telephone.

Totally exhausted and wanting nothing more than to be left alone, Mia forced herself to get out of bed and pick up the handset on the other side of the room.

"So, is it true you hooked up with that jerk cop again? Morgan said he saw you and Foxe leaving the health center together last night. You weren't just working out together, were you?"

Mia winced at Courtney's angry voice. She'd spent a lot of time complaining to her best friend about Colin.

"There was a bit more to it than exercising," she admitted.

"Why?"

Mia almost felt guilty when she answered. "It just happened. We were mugged, or maybe it was carjackers—"

"What? Are you all right?"

She ached all over, but not from being in a fight. "I'm fine." Her memory was a little fuzzy on the exact details of what had happened in the garage. "We were attacked by three or four guys. And this is embarrassing, but I totally reacted like a girl—let Colin defend my honor, or whatever—"

"You? The kick-ass martial arts queen?"

"It's true. I don't know why. It's almost as embarrassing as letting him bring me home and—"

"You slept with him? Out of gratitude?"

Mia squirmed. "Why are you abusing me this early in the day?"

"Somebody needs to abuse you. You have no control where that jerk is involved. I cannot believe that you let him stay the night."

Mia sighed. "He didn't stay."

"Well, isn't that typical? What does that tell you about him? Couldn't he stay the night and be comforting in case you were upset?"

Mia didn't disagree with her friend's harsh criticism. "At least he *was* here. He has many faults, but the desire was mutual—this adrenaline thing kicked in. It's not as if we thought about it; there's this almost perverted, animalistic—"

"Oh, yeah?" Courtney sounded almost amused. "What'd you do?"

Mia looked at her body, thinking she'd see a

few bruises from the wild sex, but her flesh was unmarked, even though aching muscles told a different story. "I vaguely remember a lot of scratching and biting, but maybe I did all that. And I'm not telling you any more."

"Listen, hon, even if the sex was great, you can't let him break your heart again. You told me to tell you that if you ever saw him again."

"I know." Hell, the man wasn't here, and it hurt that he wasn't here. Last week she'd halfway thought that she might someday get over him. Now this *hunger* she had for Colin Foxe was back in full force. She was such a fool. "Maybe I shouldn't have had sex with him, but—"

She couldn't explain her reactions to Colin, not when the gut lust he caused sometimes overrode her higher brain function. Last night had been completely out of control, for both of them, she was certain. She didn't think they'd made it to the bedroom, even if she'd woken up in her bed. Alone. It was disturbing not to know how she'd gotten from there to here, or when Colin had left.

"He didn't say good-bye."

"That's typical."

"Yeah," she agreed, though she'd been talking to herself rather than to Courtney.

But she was more disturbed by the holes in her memory, and by the nagging worry that something wasn't right, than she was by her friend's comments. Dream images flashed through her mind, mixed in with what she could remember from last night. Which wasn't as much as she should.

She rubbed a hand across her face. She just didn't feel right. "I'm really not awake, Courtney. Let's meet for lunch and talk about it later, okay?"

She hung up before Courtney could answer, and went to take a shower.

Hot water helped, but she could still feel Colin's touch on her body. The hot water also helped clear her foggy mind. Memories and actions fell into place as she scrubbed herself vigorously with almond-scented bath gel.

She remembered the flight back from Colorado. It took her a while longer to remember why she'd been to Colorado in the first place. In fact, for a few minutes she firmly believed the notion that vampires were real was a ridiculous dream.

For a few minutes she was frightened that she was crazy.

When she closed her eyes and let the water pound against her face and throat, memories of the attack last night came back to her. Except, one set of memories kept overlaying another.

In one image—the one that insisted it was the real memory—she watched Colin fight off a group of carjackers in a dark garage.

The other images were far more chaotic and crowded, and buried beneath the more logical attack. There were monsters in these memories. Not only monsters, but more people. She and Colin hadn't been alone. She still hadn't been much use—that shameful memory was real—but other good guys had ridden to the rescue in a big black SUV.

For a moment she could almost make out the license plate number of a Lincoln Navigator, but the image faded and wouldn't come back.

"Damn." She struck a fist against the wet tiles of the shower wall. "Remember!"

The vampire attack was the truth, wasn't it?

Yep. Reality was the scary, weird stuff.

Why had her subconscious tried to fool her into thinking otherwise?

She supposed that the trauma of facing real vampires was just more than she'd been prepared for, even if she'd thought she was ready.

Or maybe vampires kept their existence secret by telepathically projecting false memories at people. Her great-grandfather had mentioned that the monsters had hypnotic powers. The vampires projecting false images at her and Colin as they fled made as much sense as the changed memories being trauma-induced. More, if she wanted to believe she wasn't going just plain crazy.

But the brainwashing hadn't lasted long. She was glad that the real memories surfaced so quickly, even though she was left standing in the shower shaking from them. Well, she wasn't exactly glad—but concentrating on vampires would keep her mind off Colin. She left the shower, and dressed.

She was in the kitchen with a mug of green tea cupped in her hands before she thought of the rescue squad again. She squinted, trying to recall exactly what they'd done and said, but those memories remained blurred.

They'd shown up . . . maybe they'd already been chasing the vampires. They had to be official vampire hunters, and she needed to hook up with them.

One of them was named Tony, she recalled. He drove my car home.

That's right. Colin brought her home in his car, and the other man followed. The men had argued about something in the driveway, but she couldn't remember what.

And it didn't matter, because she'd just thought of a way to find Tony. After all, she did have a backup team of sorts she'd been told she could call on.

Mia put down her tea and picked up the kitchen phone. She called her great-grandfather's high-powered attorney. "Can you help me find out a man's identity from his fingerprints?" she asked.

Mia smiled when she was told that it was possible. Her addiction to all the CSI crime dramas on television had paid off.

Chapter Nine

"You made her forget *everything* about last night?"

Colin did not take kindly to Alec Reynard's tone. "That's not what I said," he replied.

He sat back in the small booth and took a sip of beer. They were in a bar in downtown Los Angeles that catered to customers of a supernatural nature, so there was no need to moderate their voices. It was the middle of the afternoon, the place was nearly empty, and the two vampires had met for an information exchange.

Colin would have preferred to be watching over Mia, but it was judged that she was safe in the daylight. They also kept telling him it wasn't his job, and Alec had demanded a briefing on Colin's activities after Tony left.

Alec looked concerned at Colin's answer. "What exactly *did* you do?"

"I just rearranged her memories."

The older vampire shook his head. "I'm not sure that's a good idea."

Colin didn't want his cousin's advice, but part of Prime training was to at least listen to the so-called wisdom of one's elders, especially Primes of one's own clan. He and Alec were both Reynard Clan, though from different lines and houses. Besides, Alec was buying the beer.

Colin took another sip from his cold bottle of Corona and grudgingly asked, "Why not?"

"I tried messing with Domini's mind and memories when we first met. I thought it would be best if she forgot any weird stuff she encountered." He shook his head. "It didn't take."

"This will take, and I was very careful."

Though maybe he had been in a bit of a hurry. Touching Mia's mind was as arousing as touching her body. He hadn't gone deeply into her subconscious, just far enough in to overlay and rearrange memories. Then he'd gotten out of her head and house before giving in to the temptation to rouse the sleeping woman and have sex with her again.

"Besides, Mia's not like Domini," Colin pointed out. "Domini was born to be one of us. Mia is merely human."

"Merely?" Sarcasm was thick in Alec's voice.

"Don't start with me." Colin cut off the lecture he knew was coming. "I took my vows. I take of mortals' bodies and blood, but they are not my kind. I care for Mia, but she's—"

"Not your kind? You racist pig."

"You can be as pissed off as you want, but I made my choice the first time I attended a Convocation of the Clans. I don't remember what serious stuff the Matri and elders met about, but I do remember the partying, and what it was like to be surrounded by all those beautiful, mysterious, sensual Clan women. Bonding with a mortal woman is fine for other Primes, but it is not for me," Colin told his cousin.

"You're saying that you think bonding with a mortal woman is second best?" Alec sounded dangerously annoyed.

Colin ignored Alec's politically correct attitude. "I'm saying that I want *our* life, to live within *our* culture, to bond with a Clan female, to be the father of her house."

Alec was thoughtful for a moment, then shrugged off his annoyance. "Okay. I agree that's not a bad life to aspire to."

"It's what all of us really want and need, no matter how much time we spend among mortal kind. It's nature's joke on us that there are more Primes than there are females, so not all Primes can have a vampire mate. In the old days, we

Primes could at least fight each other to the death over mating rights to our women. It cut the male population, and it was good for the gene pool."

Alec laughed. "I'm glad the Matri Council outlawed that practice centuries ago. Though I certainly don't mind a nice first-blood fight over a woman—or I didn't, until I found my bondmate."

"That kind of combat's one hell of an aphrodisiac." Colin finished his beer. "I thought Flare was quite impressed when I blooded Kiril at the Convocation last year."

"Did she sleep with you?"

"No."

"Then my sister wasn't impressed. Don't tell me you want to bond with Flare. She's restless and bad-tempered and mean."

"You only think that because she's your sister. She's hot. Very, very hot. Our women are pure fire, compared to fragile mortal women."

Except for Mia.

Colin pushed the thought of her out of his head, though his body grew taut with memories. He made himself think about vampire women.

"I don't know which one I want yet. Maybe Flare, maybe Maja, or Chaviva—there's a dozen or so to choose from. I've got years before I need to make up my mind, before the bonding urge strikes between me and a Clan woman. In the meantime—" Colin smiled lecherously and held his arms wide, taking in the whole city. "So many mortal women, so very much time."

Oddly enough, the only mortal image that came to mind was Mia, and he didn't feel as enthusiastic about many future decades of casual mating as he should.

He changed the subject. "I checked out the lead at the Van Trier airport yesterday, before all hell broke loose with the Mia incident."

Alec leaned eagerly forward across the table. "Did you find out anything? Are we any closer to this Patron? I'd like to know a name instead of having to use this pretentious Patron crap."

Colin grinned. "Yeah. We Primes are the only ones allowed pretentious titles."

"We've earned that right over thousands of years of tradition. This Patron is just some creep trying to live off of us. And he's willing to kill to do it, both our kind *and* mortals. I hate that it's taking so long to track him down."

"You don't have to remind me," Colin said. "I was there, at his Arizona lab facility. I'm the one who let him get away," he added, angry at himself.

"Did you find anything useful at the airport?"

"I got an address for a law firm that leased

hangar space for a Gulfstream for a client. The lease was for two years, but the plane hasn't flown in or out of Van Trier for a while. Since we have the Patron's Gulfstream hidden away in Arizona, *it* also hasn't been flown out of Van Trier."

"Sounds like it could be the same one."

"I need to check out this law firm. Or maybe it would be better for someone else to follow this lead. I'm not a detective; my job's to hunt the Patron when we discover who he is. And Mia—"

Colin's head came up sharply, words lost as all his sense focused on Mia. She was—somewhere.

Somewhere she wasn't supposed to be. Doing something she shouldn't be doing. With someone else. With a male.

Colin growled deep in his throat and left the bar, totally intent on finding Mia.

As she sat on a bench on a shaded sidewalk in Santa Monica and gazed at the one-story, hacienda-style apartment complex across the street, Mia wasn't sure what to do next.

Oh, she knew what she had to do; it was finding the right approach that was giving her trouble. Marching up to the door and ringing the bell, rather than calling first, had seemed like a good idea until she got here. But now she wondered if the direct approach was the correct one.

She now knew that Tony's full name was Anthony Crowe. He was a retired homicide detective with LAPD, with a brilliant service record and lots of commendations. He owned the renovated 1930s building, where he had resided for twenty years.

Though the man she remembered didn't look old enough to be retired. She hadn't noticed any gray in his black hair or beard. Of course it had been dark, and her memories still wove in and out of two very different scenarios, unless she concentrated hard enough to get a headache.

Maybe he'd been seriously injured in the line of duty and forced to retire early. There was always a nagging worry in the back of her mind that something awful would happen to Colin, though he naturally thought he was indestructible. She guessed that Colin knew Tony from the police connection.

Mia reminded herself sternly that she hadn't tracked down Tony Crowe to discuss Colin Foxe—

Foxe. Foxe and—Crowe.

What an interesting coincidence that both men had animal names. And hadn't her great-grandfather said that vampires ran in packs and used animal names? Though the only group he'd mentioned specifically called themselves the Snakes.

How charming.

Crowe and Foxe were relatively common names, though, and crows and foxes were fairly harmless creatures. Her revved-up nerves were creating connections out of simple coincidences.

She'd been sitting on this bench for a good half hour, stalling like this. She didn't know why approaching Crowe was harder for her than finding her grandfather.

Except, maybe, for the insidious voice in her head that kept telling her there were things she shouldn't know, shadows she could not explore, secrets meant to be kept.

That voice sounded a lot like Colin's, and it was beginning to piss her off.

The voice only grew stronger as she forced herself to rise and cross the street. A low stucco wall with a decorative iron gate separated a gardened courtyard from the sidewalk. The gate wasn't locked, so Mia went inside. A small tiled fountain bubbled in the center of the courtyard. Mia paused as a pair of startled doves took flight off the rim of the fountain, then marched up to a dark, carved wooden door and rang the doorbell.

A male voice said, "Yes?" through an intercom a few moments later.

"Mr. Crowe?"

"Yes," he answered cautiously after a pause.

"My name is Caramia Luchese. You don't know me, but we met last night. You know where, and why," she added.

The door opened, and a man who was distinctly not a senior citizen, but *was* Tony from last night, stood in the doorway. "Miss Luchese," he said. "I get the distinct feeling that you have no concept of leaving well enough alone." There was an amused twinkle in his eyes, but that didn't stop him from looking extremely dangerous.

"How can I leave well enough alone when it concerns me?" she answered.

"Does Colin know you're here?"

"Colin, has nothing to do with this," she answered, confused and annoyed.

"Really?" he questioned, coolly amused. He smiled, and looked her up and down in a way that made her flushed and flustered. "How did you find me? And is it me you want? And would you like to come inside to explain it all?"

His voice was a rich purr, and Mia felt like Little Red Riding Hood invited into the Big Bad Wolf's den.

She gestured toward a table and chairs set on a brick patio beneath a pair of palm trees, suddenly feeling that discussing vampires out in the open might be best.

"Why don't we talk over there?"

"Sweetheart, we shouldn't be talking at all."

She didn't like the endearment from a stranger, but let it go. She also didn't like it when he took her arm and led her over to the shaded patio, then waited until she was seated before he said, "Would you like some lemonade? Cookies?"

"There's a certain smug amusement to your gallantry, Mr. Crowe," she answered, keeping her tone calm. "I don't understand that."

"Oh, it's a Prime thing." He glanced toward the street, then at his watch. Then he sat in the other chair after moving it closer to hers, though this put him directly in the bright sunlight. "We have a few minutes to get to know each other. Tell me everything you know."

She looked at him suspiciously. She wasn't sure how she expected this confrontation to go, but the man's confident amusement was unsettling. "Everything I know about what?"

"Vampires, of course. And not just the monsters that have been pursuing you. Do you know why they're after you?"

"No, I don't know—wait a minute."

She'd come to get information from him, and he was attempting to control the information, to learn from her rather than tell her anything.

"What do you know about vampire hunters?" she asked, keeping stubbornly to her own agenda.

"How do I get in touch with them? Are you one?"

"Vampire or hunter?"

She smiled. "Sorry, I phrased that poorly."

"Not necessarily."

"Is Colin a hunter?"

"He's definitely a predator." He gave her an assessing look. "More than he knows, I think."

Mia hated her unconscious rush to bring Colin into every conversation, especially after months of trying to do a memory dump of the man. But he'd come back into her life at the same time the vampires showed up, and she couldn't believe it was a coincidence.

"When we were attacked last night, Colin wanted me to believe that the monsters are a human cult. But he was just trying to protect me, wasn't he?"

She wasn't sure if she was going to be pleased or furious if she found out that Colin Foxe was the very thing she was looking for.

"I think he very much wants to protect your life," Crowe answered. "And that he's trying to protect himself, as well."

"How is he involved in this? How are you?"

"I'm always fine, darlin'."

First *sweetheart*, now *darlin'*. She could tell he was trying to rile her, and tried hard not to show her annoyance.

"You know what I meant."

"How am I involved with vampires, you mean, rather than the state of my health?" He leaned closer and chuckled. The sound was low and sexy. "I'm involved in every way possible."

"Get away from her, Corvus."

Mia sprang to her feet at the threatening sound of Colin's voice. Tony rose as well, laughing, and turned to face Colin. Mia had to move a few steps sideways to see past Tony Crowe's broad shoulders. Colin's face was a mask of fury. Every whipcord lean muscle was taut, as though he was just barely holding himself back from attacking the other man.

"What are you doing here?" she asked Colin.

"What are *you* doing here?" he demanded, but he directed most of his anger at Tony. "What do you think you're doing?"

"I was waiting to see how quickly you'd show up, Reynard."

"Did you think I'd let you do whatever you please with my—"

"Your what?"

"My—" Colin pointed. "Her."

"Is she is, or is she ain't?"

Crowe smiled, and he seemed to have very sharp teeth all of a sudden. Colin took a step closer.

Though she saw two men facing off in the hot afternoon sunlight, Mia had a strong impression of watching a pair of leashed fighting beasts getting ready to go at each other with fangs and claws and hard male muscle. A shiver of fear went through her, like an ice cube being run down her spine. She wanted to run, and she didn't like the sensation. Before being chased by the vampires last night, she'd never backed down from any challenge. She couldn't be a coward again. Besides, it seemed this confrontation was somehow over her.

She cleared her throat. "Excuse me, but—"

"Stay out of this," both men said at once.

"Screw you," was her automatic defiance at this high-handedness. "I'm not being fought over like a piece of meat."

She always got reckless when her temper flared, but she didn't turn her back on the men as she edged away from the patio. They seemed momentarily stunned by her words, and while they stared, she moved toward the courtyard gate. She was almost ready to break into a sprint when a hand landed on her shoulder, bringing her to an abrupt stop.

"Don't run," a voice warned her.

When she turned around, she saw Alec from the garage rescue party. The woman called

Domini came up to join him a moment later. Then Colin and Crowe were there, as well. Mia had the impression of being surrounded by a pride of hungry lions.

"Back off, boys," Domini said.

Surprisingly, the men all took a step back. Yet that didn't make Mia feel any less trapped.

"What's up?" Domini asked.

Tony answered, "I think our young Prime has gotten the girl in trouble." He looked at Alec. "Can't you *smell* what's going on between them?"

"What are you talking about?" Mia and Colin demanded at the same time.

Tony chuckled and shook his head. "They haven't got a clue."

"To what?" Domini asked.

"Just look at them, hon," Alec told her. "With all your senses."

"Oh," she said after a moment.

"Do you know what I think?" Tony asked. "I think we take them to the Matri. Right now."

Chapter Ten

The room was decorated in a luxurious, *Arabian Nights* harem way, with a big bed, a thick Persian carpet, a sitting area with a pair of comfortable chairs and a full bookcase, and a marble fantasy bathroom. But there were no windows, and she'd been locked in.

She'd been kidnapped, firmly but politely taken away by the people who'd come to the rescue the night before. Her only consolation was that Colin had been abducted as well. They'd been put in different cars and brought to a secluded mansion hours before. She hadn't seen him since they'd stepped inside the house.

A group of men had taken him away; several older women had joined Domini and escorted Mia to her nicely appointed prison. Domini looked concerned, but everyone else's expressions had been neutral or downright hostile. Mia got the impression that they found her presence thoroughly inconvenient.

She'd been left alone for a while, then Domini came in and introduced her to a Dr. Casmerek. He'd wanted blood and urine samples. Of course she'd refused, in a very physical way. She'd tried to get past Domini to get to the door, and almost made it. But Domini was unnaturally fast and strong, and the combination of aikido and Krav Maga fighting techniques she used took Mia by surprise. The woman's unconventional style didn't make her give up, though.

The doctor stayed out of the way until the fight was over. A few things got broken; Mia hoped they were priceless antiques.

Mia ended up grudgingly giving him the fluid samples, but she was pleased that at least she'd put up a fight, at least *tried* to control the situation.

Domini smiled at her and said, "You did good," before she followed the doctor out, leaving Mia alone in the locked room once more.

What sort of medical tests was this Dr. Casmerek running on her?

Mia paced while she fretted. Every now and then she paused to listen at the door, or to pick up a piece of broken porcelain or glass. After a while she had a nice little collection piled on a table. None of them were large enough or sharp enough to make a decent weapon, but at least thinking about it helped.

She didn't know exactly where Colin was, but she had the feeling he was close by—she almost believed she could find him if she could get out of the room. The weirdest thing was, she thought she could feel him wanting to be with her. She'd had sensations like this about him before, but never as strongly as now.

And what good would finding him do her? Though it would be kind of fun to be the one who came to the rescue this time.

And then he could explain to her what was going on. He knew these people, thought he hadn't seemed very lucid when he showed up at Tony Crowe's. And he'd been just as confused and outraged as she was by the others' actions.

Was Dr. Casmerek running tests on him, too?

And what did Colin's mood swings and their being kidnapped have to do with vampires?

After a while she picked a book at random from the case and settled on one of the deep, comfortable chairs. It was a big, heavy book, with fine leather binding. She was contemplating how she might be able to use it to smash someone if she waited by the door when the door opened silently across the room.

Mia swore under her breath at the lost opportunity and rose to her feet as Domini came in, followed by Alec.

"Sorry to have kept you waiting so long," Alec said.

As kidnappers went, these people were certainly polite.

"The matris will see you now," Alec said.

"The what?" Mia asked. "Where's Colin? Is he all right?"

The man and woman exchanged an infuriatingly knowing glance.

"He might not be when the matris get through with him," Alec answered. "They wish to see you, as well," he went on.

His tone implied that there was no questioning the wishes of this Matris person or persons. All Mia cared about was getting out of this room and finally finding out what was going on. And, all right, she wanted Colin. His presence wasn't always necessarily reassuring, but it was— important—to her.

"Fine," she said. "Lead on."

Mia walked toward the door, but Domini put a hand on her arm before she could leave.

"One thing," she said. "The medical tests came back. The good news is that you're not pregnant. At least, I assume you take it as good news."

Mia flushed deeply, appalled and embarrassed. She shook off the woman's touch. "I didn't ask to take any tests," she reminded Domini. And what was the bad news? she wondered. Were they testing her for some sort of disease? She was too proud, and scared, to ask.

"I don't mean to seem rude," Domini said. "And of course you don't think this is any of our business, but believe me, it really is for your own good."

"And Colin's," Alec added. "Shall we?" He gestured toward the door.

All Colin could do was pace like a trapped animal back and forth across the thickly carpeted bedroom, which got boring very quickly. He'd been furious when they'd brought him to the Citadel, and his mood hadn't gotten any better in the long hours since.

No windows. The door was guarded. Other people were allowed in and out, but Colin Foxe was trapped in another clan's stronghold.

He was angry at this intrusion into his privacy. He was impatient at the interruption of the hunt for the Patron. He was annoyed that Mia had been brought to the Shagal house, and even more angry that he was not allowed to see her. He was infuriated at the long hours he'd been made to wait, all but a prisoner in a guest room, without any explanation.

Even the usually forthright Dr. Casmerek had refused to tell him anything, other than to say that the blood he wanted from Colin was for tests.

What sort of tests? None of this made any sense. What by the devils of darkness had his involvement with Mia gotten him into?

And worst of all, when lovely Cassiopeia, Matri Serisa's only daughter and heir, had come into the bedroom and offered to spend the night in his bed, he hadn't even been interested. She was a beautiful, sensual, exciting vampire woman who no Prime in his right mind would turn down. Yet Colin had barely been able to keep his rejection polite enough not to cause offense.

"What is the matter with me?" he asked, turning to face Anthony Crowe as the door opened and the other Prime came into the room.

"We're scheduled to discuss exactly what's wrong with you," Tony answered.

"I turned down Cassie Shagal," Colin went on. "Can you believe that?"

He was totally stunned at his uncharacteristic behavior. He wasn't going to ask himself why. What he needed was to get out of here, get away from all this Clan crap, and get his head together on his own.

"Can I go now?" he demanded.

"Not yet."

"There are rules against this kind of treatment!"

"Yep. But there are extenuating circumstances that have to be worked out involving you and Miss Mia."

"Have you sent Mia home? Did Matri Serisa make her forget about us?"

That would be the best thing for her, even if Colin did resent anyone else touching Mia's mind but him. If he let himself think that perhaps some Prime had probed the mortal woman's thoughts, he knew a jealous red rage would overtake him. He did not want to be jealous of Mia. He wouldn't let himself be.

He took a deep breath, and made himself say, "I'm sorry I acted like I did at your place. There was no reason for it. Was there?" he added, as jealousy shot through him once more.

Tony shook his head and looked at him steadily for a moment before he said, "A few things have to be settled before you two can leave. Come on."

Colin suddenly caught his breath on a scent, a sense.

"Mia."

Colin pushed out of the room ahead of Tony. Though he hadn't been able to feel her presence for hours, he was now keenly aware that she was close by. But there were two other Primes waiting in the hall, and Tony at his back.

He was ready to start a brawl with all three to get to Mia, but she appeared around a corner and ran toward him a moment later. He had her in his arms before he noticed Alec and Domini following her. Tony grabbed him and pulled him back before he could kiss Mia, then Domini stepped between them.

"Hey!" Mia complained.

"Hands off!" Colin shouted. He was surprised when Tony let him go. The problem was now getting around Domini, since there was no way he would use force on a woman.

"No way," Domini said before he could think up a plea or a cajoling word. "Serisa——"

"Actually, there is a slight change of plans," Tony broke in. "Serisa and the other ladies want these two to have a little talk before they get on with other matters."

Colin spun to face Tony. "Talk? I don't want to talk to the woman."

"What?" Mia asked indignantly behind him.

He turned back to her. "I want to get you safely back home," he explained.

He could tell she was scared, and covering it

up with her usual bravado. The others couldn't see it, or didn't care, but he knew that Mia was upset.

"She might be home," Domini said.

Colin hadn't a clue what Alec's bondmate meant.

"Who's Serisa? And what does she want us to talk about?" Mia shot a look at Domini. "What do you mean, I might be home?"

It occurred to Colin that Mia was following the enigmatic thread of conversation better than he was. She was no fool. Out of her depth, of course, but sharp.

"Don't worry, you will get explanations," Tony told Mia. He concentrated on Colin. "But first Serisa wants you to explain everything about us to her. *Everything,*" he added firmly. "Truth first," he added, with one of his annoying grins, "then consequences."

"The truth?" Colin was appalled. "She can't handle the truth!"

"Aaron Sorkin, *A Few Good Men,*" Domini muttered. When everyone stared at her, she smiled at Alec, then focused her attention on Colin. "I handled the truth, didn't I?"

"But you're one of us," Colin objected.

"I wasn't then."

"Yes, but—"

"Will you people stop arguing, and tell me what's going on?" Mia demanded.

Colin hated that every gaze was on them. Even worse, Mia's needs called to him all tangled up with his own.

"Fine," he finally agreed. "She's going to have to forget it all, but I'll tell her."

"Everything," Tony admonished. "Including what you've done to her."

"*What* have you done to me?" Mia asked.

Colin was far too aware of the crowd. "Not here."

Tony pointed toward the bedroom. Colin grabbed Mia's hand and hustled her inside. This time he was glad when the door shut behind them.

Once they were alone, he turned to her and gave her the blunt truth.

"I'm a vampire."

Chapter Eleven

"$\mathcal{N}$o, you're not."

Her response certainly wasn't unexpected, but Colin couldn't help but be indignant. "What do you mean, No, you're not? I ought to know what I am: a vampire Prime of Clan Reynard."

She shook off his hand and backed away to look him up and down. "That's not possible."

Colin did his best to see the situation through her eyes, and tried to sound soothing. "I realize that you're confused."

"Oh, yes, I'm confused. But don't try to tell me that you're a vampire."

"It's not only me," he told her. "Everyone in the house is a vampire. Except Domini, and maybe a couple of the Primes' mortal bondmates, but they're special cases." He sighed, and held up a hand. "Never mind, I'm going too fast. Let's concentrate on you and me, and get this over with."

"Yes," she said. "Let's."

There was a gleam of anger in her eyes and in her spirit that stabbed at him. Maybe he was choosing his words wrongly, not being tactful enough. It was hard to tell with women. They were hard to talk to, but he'd been told to be honest.

"You've seen vampires," he reminded her. "I tried to make you forget that we exist."

There was a long moment where the sense of anger and betrayal sizzled around her, but she got it under control. "It didn't work. Not for long, anyway."

He was surprised by her mental resilience, and rather proud of her, despite the inconvenience. "That's the trouble with trying to manipulate psychics," he explained. "You can never be certain it's going to work. You seem to be getting stronger. What did you do, go to Tony when the false memories wore off? And why Tony? How'd you find him?"

A stubborn mask came over her features, and her mind. "Aren't you the one who's supposed to be doing the talking?"

"There's plenty of things you need to answer for."

"You first."

Her tone cut like a knife.

More than that, it excited him. Every fiery look from her, every word, stimulated him more. Though the passion that seethed inside her was from anger, Colin knew instinctively how to channel and change it to the kind of passion that brought pleasure, and completion.

"Mia. We can do better things than fight." His voice was full of sultry promise. He took a step toward his beautiful human, reaching for her. She gasped when his fingers touched the side of her throat and slid across her shoulders, and the familiar, delicious crackle of desire passed between them.

Then she danced away to the far side of the room. She held her hands up before her when he would have followed. "I don't make love to vampires."

He smiled and glanced toward the king-sized bed in the center of the room. Just because they were stuck in here didn't mean they couldn't have some fun. He nodded toward it, all cocky and sure of himself. Mia always came to him in the end, no matter how much they fought.

"Then maybe I won't confess to being one."

"Good. Because—"

"But that would be a lie. And I'm told that's not allowed."

He sat down on the end of the bed and patted the spot next to him for her to join him. "You've been making love to a vampire for months, Mia. Come and make love to one again."

Mia slowly turned her back on Colin, though she could still feel his gaze on her. For hours all she'd wanted was to be with him, but now she couldn't bear to look at him. But that didn't keep the memories from rising up to haunt her through all the layers of confusion.

She didn't take strangers home; she wasn't that kind of woman—but here they were in her bedroom, with no more conversation than the words they'd exchanged in the hospital. Somehow he knew the way to her home, into the most private place where she lived. She welcomed him into this sanctuary, and gave herself up to the desire that had been waiting for him to kindle.

He didn't touch her like a stranger, but as the lover who knew and fulfilled her every desire. When she touched him, she knew every hard-muscled inch of him. The scent and heat and taste of him was a homecoming rather than a revelation.

They were meant to fit together, and they did, falling onto the bed, ripping off each other's clothes, moving together, mouths and hands finding all the right places with frantic, fulfilling urgency. There was no gentleness in this coupling; they both rode the wildness, loved it. There were moments of pain that only intensified the pleasure. They clawed at each other as he thrust into her. Clawed and scratched and—

Bit.

Mia touched her right breast, as the memory of the first time it happened washed over her with erotic intensity that almost sent her to her knees.

"You *bit* me."

"Upon occasion."

How could he sound so damned smug?

She whirled around and glared at Colin. His biting *her* wasn't the only thing she remembered about their wild lovemaking, but she wasn't ready to face the rest of it.

"You bit me!"

"I tasted you," he corrected. "That's what we call it. We never take more than a few drops of blood at a time, but it heightens our partner's pleasure, and ours. You remember the pleasure, but not what we do."

How could he say that, when she was remembering it right now? She also remembered the taste of copper in her mouth. "You are so obtuse, Colin Foxe."

"But I'm sexy."

Sex *had* been the basis of their relationship. But sex with a vampire? Her stomach twisted at the thought.

"Biting me doesn't make you a vampire," she said. "And vampires aren't sexy. Except maybe Angel and Spike, but they're fictional. Real vampires are monsters. I've been attacked by them."

"Tribe vampires are monsters. I'm Clan."

Tribe. Clan. Family. She'd heard the terms. Her great-grandfather had told her that vampires divided themselves into three distinct types. He'd also told her that the distinctions made no difference. Vampires of any type were inimical parasites, meant to be killed by humans. That Colin knew about the different kinds of vampires frightened her.

"Is this some kind of test? I'm trying to find vampire hunters, but when I think I find the hunters, I'm told they're vampires. That doesn't make sense."

Colin stood up slowly, and he looked very annoyed. "What do you want with hunters?"

"Vampires have been attacking me," she reminded him.

This calmed him a little. "How do you know about the hunters?"

She wasn't ready to answer this. "I've seen you in the sunlight. Vampires can't bear the light."

She remembered being with him on the beach on the hottest day of the year. She remembered making love at midday in her garden, laughing about getting their butts burned if they weren't careful. They'd rubbed coconut-scented sunblock all over each other. She remembered the way his skin felt, slick with the cream and warmed by the sun.

And she remembered talking to Tony Crowe in his courtyard, how he'd turned his face up to the clear California sky. And how Colin and he had faced off in the middle of the bright Los Angeles afternoon.

"How can you all be vampires when you run around in the daylight?"

"We take drugs. Lots of drugs. This is the twenty-first century, woman. Do you think we haven't changed with the times?"

That was one of the things her great-grandfather wanted to know. That's why he wanted a live vampire to study. Maybe she should take Colin to her great-grandfather.

And if she could think like that, it must mean that she was beginning to believe he really was a vampire. Which would mean . . .

That she'd been sleeping with the enemy.

A wave of self-loathing overtook her, strong enough to drive her to her knees. Colin was beside her almost before she hit the floor. Then his hands were on her.

"Monster!" she shouted. "Get your hands off me, you disgusting parasite!"

He backed off, and there was hurt in his voice when he said, "Hey!"

She looked up at him, realized she was on her knees in front of a vampire, and got to her feet. She wasn't going to show weakness in front of him—in front of *it*. Looking at him, even knowing what he was—what he proudly proclaimed to be—she still had trouble seeing past the man she'd cared for to the beast he truly was.

It made it worse that she couldn't look at him without wanting him. She'd have to put the yearning down to some sort of telepathic glamor he exerted on her, which made her want him. Because if wanting him was something that came from inside her, then she was a weak, perverted fool.

Mia was looking at him as if she'd never seen him before, and Colin accepted that. What ground on his temper was that she radiated intense hatred and anger—not only at him, but at herself. What was that about?

Maybe she wanted him to apologize for what he was, which was not going to happen. "I'm proud of being a vampire. We're faster, stronger, longer-lived, and have better sight, hearing, and vision than humans. We're psychic as hell."

She sneered. "You're better than humans, is that it?"

"The Clans are protectors of humans, Mia. We look after your kind."

"My *kind*. What arrogance." She crossed her arms. "And what's the bill for being so tenderly looked after by your superior species? Do you do it for free?"

"Yes, of course. Well—"

"Do you look after us like shepherds with their flocks?"

"Yeah," he answered. "Like that."

"Sheep end up being slaughtered, Foxe. They're protected until the shepherd decides they make a tasty stew."

"Oh, come on!"

"How many people have you slaughtered?"

"I'm a *cop*."

"Cops kill people, and get away with it. What a great cover for a vampire. Didn't you just shoot a couple of bank robbers in the line of duty?" She laughed bitterly. "And to think I was worried about how you reacted to killing those men. How many innocent peoples' blood have you taken while wearing the uniform?"

For now he'd accept that in her ignorance she could ridicule what it meant to be a Clan Prime. But there was no way he let her get away with accusing him of being a bad cop!

Colin took a furious step toward her, only to spin toward the door when it opened.

"Time's up," Tony Crowe announced.

Chapter Twelve

"Not now!" Colin shouted at Crowe.

Mia was relieved to have Colin's attention diverted from her. The wild look in his eyes when he came toward her had scared her. She'd never been frightened by him before, and she cursed herself for rousing the temper of a monster when she didn't yet know how to defend herself against him.

Damn it! Why hadn't her great-grandfather been more helpful? Why hadn't she found the human vampire hunters before running into this nest of monsters?

She was such a fool for mistaking Colin, Tony, and all the rest for hunters just because they'd fought off the other vampires. Had she stumbled into the middle of some territorial dispute?

"I'm just the messenger," Tony answered Colin. "Did you tell her about us?"

"I've been trying to. She just called me a bad cop. A Prime has to defend his honor."

Tony gave her a disapproving look. "We're very proud that he qualified for SWAT at his tender age."

"He's thirty-two," Mia said. At least that's what he'd told her—as if anything Colin Foxe said about himself was true.

"They let you out of the crèche awfully young, didn't they?" Tony said to Colin.

"I'm old enough to kick your ass, old-timer."

"I might let you try, pup." Tony came farther into the room, and looked Mia up and down in a way that made her blush. "But you know what you'd be giving up if I won. I'm a hundred and three," he added to Mia. "Think of all the experience I have to offer you."

"Hey!" Colin put himself between Mia and the other vampire.

"Enough," a woman's voice said from behind them. "Anthony, be good." A small, dignified woman swept into the room, commanding everyone's attention with her regal manner. She bent a stern look on Mia that made her feel about five years old before she addressed Tony again. "Unless you mean to rescue this young woman from an untenable situation."

"Should the need arise, Lady Serisa, it will be a privilege."

"Good. Come along. We've been waiting to settle this long enough."

Serisa left, and they all followed without a word. Colin reached for her hand as they walked down a wide hallway, but Mia sharply snatched it away.

Don't touch me!

Fine.

Mia realized that neither of them had spoken aloud. Telepathy? It made sense that a vampire was a telepath, but how could she send thoughts to him, as well? Come to think of it, she remembered hearing his voice in her head even before they met, telling her to calm down. How had he gotten into her head like that? How did she get into his?

She had to put her speculations on hold when they entered a large room full of people. Full of vampires—just because they looked like people didn't mean they were. They were all attractive and well dressed, though mostly in black. They were all staring at her.

A tall, barrel-chested man came forward. He had gray at his temples and deep lines around his eyes. When he spoke, his voice was deep and mellow. "I am Barak, elder of Clan Shagal. Welcome to our Citadel." He glanced toward the woman. "Serisa is my lady. She is Matri here."

Then he smiled at Mia, and the expression in

his gaze was so kindly and concerned that it left her wishing that Barak was her great-grandfather. She couldn't help but smile back.

He took her hand and made sure she was seated comfortably in a deep black leather chair on one side of the room. Then he moved to stand in front of Colin.

"Sit," Barak ordered him brusquely.

"I'll stand," Colin answered. He looked around the crowded room. "This looks like a trial. What am I being accused of?"

The atmosphere in the room grew even tenser as Barak and Colin stared at each other for a few moments. When Barak nodded and Colin came striding past him to stand next to her, people relaxed. There were even approving looks and a few smiles when he put his hand on her shoulder. Mostly, Mia was aware of the comfort that came from contact with Colin in the midst of all these strangers.

She looked up at him. "You confuse the hell out of me, Foxe."

He looked down at her. "The feeling's mutual, Luchese."

"Which brings us to the heart of the matter," Serisa said. The small woman stepped to the center of the room. "We are not dealing with accusations, but with concerns. Some facts must be verified, acknowledged, and addressed. She turned to Tony Crowe. "Thank you for bringing the situation to our attention. Perhaps you should explain what you saw that alerted you."

"Alerted him to what?" Colin questioned.

"What are we being accused of?" Mia demanded.

"Kids," Tony said, and shook his head. "This is for your own good, so shut up and let's get this over with." He addressed Serisa. "One of my impressions about the girl is that we have an amateur vampire hunter on our hands."

"Amateur!" Mia piped up indignantly. Even if it was true, this Crowe person didn't have to announce it to the world. "I came to you for help," she told him.

He smiled. "But you didn't recognize me for what I am, did you? You had no idea what Colin is, after months as his lover. He didn't tell you anything, did he? And whenever you figured anything out, he tried to make you forget, right?"

Mia couldn't help but nod, and shoot Colin an angry look.

Tony addressed Serisa once more. "The boy has her so messed up, she isn't really sure of what's going on."

"Boy!" Colin shouted. "Messed up? I've never done anything to her. Except make her forget things she isn't supposed to know. For her good, and ours," he added.

"You haven't forced your blood on her?" Barak asked.

"Of course not!"

"If she didn't have your blood in her, would the Tribe pack have decided to hunt her? If you weren't linked, would they have come after her?" Serisa questioned.

"That isn't why they're hunting me," Mia said, but everyone's attention was on Colin.

"I've tasted Mia, yes. I freely admit that I've taken her blood. But I have never, *never* shared my blood with her. I wouldn't do that with a mortal woman."

"I don't think he *thinks* he has," Tony said to Serisa.

"Yet you are certain of the mingling."

"I am."

"Why are you listening to him? I'm right here! I know what I did with Mia."

"I don't think you do," Tony replied. "I met the young lady when Alec, Domini, and I answered a call for help from Colin against a Tribe attack. My impression from the first moment was that they were bonded. I quickly came to understand that neither of them were aware of it."

"Bonded?" Colin's hand squeezed her shoulder. He was utterly stunned, and unaware that he was hurting her.

She shrugged off his touch and rose to her feet. While there was a tension in the air, she wasn't feeling physically threatened. But she did fear she was in danger of being talked to death.

"Does the term *beating around the bush* have meaning for you people?" she demanded. "You've kidnapped us, and now you're interrogating us. Why? What business is it of yours, what Colin and I did together?" Had she known he was a vampire, she certainly wouldn't have slept with him, but she wasn't going to try to claim that the sex hadn't been consensual. "Maybe he messed with my memories, maybe he bit me, but that's nobody's business but ours."

And why were they so concerned about one of their own drinking someone's blood? That was what vampires did, wasn't it?

"Besides, we broke up," she went on. "It doesn't matter anymore."

"You can't break up," Serisa said. "You're bonded."

"We aren't," Colin insisted. "It's not possible. She's human."

He sounded desperate, appalled, and this hurt Mia as though he'd slapped her. She spun to face him. "Is there something wrong with being human?"

Ignoring her, Colin stepped up to confront Serisa. "This is impossible. You can't put this on me." His expression was stricken.

Serisa's answer was cold. "I do."

Domini stepped forward. "I'm sorry no one's bothered to explain bonding to you," she said to Mia. "They forget that a mortal isn't going to automatically know what they're talking about when they speak of bonding and bondmates. Basically, you and Colin are married. You are physically, spiritually, and psychically connected."

"Don't be ridiculous," Mia snapped.

"And it's permanent," Domini added.

Part of her recognized the truth of what the other woman said, but the rest of her rejected it with almost hysterical fervor.

"I cannot be"—she couldn't bring herself to use the words *bonded* or *married*—"attached to a vampire."

"We have the blood tests to prove it," Dr. Casmerek spoke up. "You can't argue with science."

"Yes, I can," Mia said.

"I am *not* bonded with this mortal," Colin asserted. "I did not give her my blood." He glared at the doctor. "I don't care what your tests show. You're lying."

"What reason would I have to lie, Prime?"

"Can you bear to be away from her?" Tony asked. "Don't you miss him when he's gone?"

"It's more than love," Domini said. "It's a wonderful craving."

"What's so wonderful about it?" Colin demanded.

"Bonding is the most wonderful thing that can happen to a Prime," Barak said.

Colin sneered. "With a human?"

"Watch it," Alec warned. Several other males echoed this sentiment.

Mia was tempted to join the argument and defend her rights, but part of her also wanted to defend Colin. After all, whatever was going on was between them, and not this loud, outraged crowd. She forcefully reminded herself that these were *vampires*, not concerned family members. Vampire in-laws? Good Lord, what an awful thought!

If only there was some way she could sneak out unnoticed while the others argued. She began to sidle slowly away from the arguing group gathered around them.

"Wouldn't I know if I was bonded?" Colin demanded.

"Not necessarily. You wouldn't be as aware of the signs as a more mature Prime. The tests show positive, but I'm not sure how it was triggered," the vampire doctor said. "You're rather young for the biological imperative to have kicked in."

"Much too young," Barak said. "What were you thinking of?"

"It's not the sort of thing you think about," Tony said.

"I—" Colin started.

"A traumatic event could have triggered the need," Serisa cut him off. "If their minds met while she was in danger, he would have responded instinctively. His desire to protect his mate could have kicked in and accelerated the bonding process. How did you meet your bonded?"

"Hostage situation," Colin answered. "I rescued her."

Mia swung back toward him. "Hey!" She curbed her outrage to acknowledge, "He and his whole team rescued us."

Tony Crowe's arms suddenly came around her from behind. "But will he rescue you now?"

The words were a seductive whisper in her ear. He pulled her closer, making her aware of hard male muscle and inescapable strength. She didn't let her shock stop her from thrusting a heel toward his shin and her head back toward his jaw.

But Colin was there before either blow connected. She caught a glimpse of bared fangs and burning eyes; Colin's handsome features were transformed into those of a bloodthirsty animal.

The next thing she knew, she was on her hands and knees on the carpet, and her mind was full of Colin's psychic voice shouting, *She's mine!*

Her soul greeted this declaration with the harrowing knowledge that she *was* his. She belonged to Colin Foxe, a vampire who fought another monster for possession of her.

Gentle hands reached for her and helped her to stand. Domini looked into her eyes and asked, "You okay?"

Mia shook her head. "It's all my fault."

Domini glanced over her shoulder. "It's already over."

She turned Mia to face the center of the room. Colin was being held between Barak and Alec; he still looked ready to kill.

Tony Crowe stood a few feet away, looking smugly satisfied, even though a bloody cut scored his cheek. "Always a groomsman," he said with a mock sigh. "Never a groom. Are you bonded or not, Colin?" he asked.

"Mia is mine!" Colin looked around, the fire in his gaze challenging every male in the room. "She's *mine*."

"I think we were all aware of that," a new voice said. A beautiful, slender woman walked out of the shadows on the far side of the room. She put a hand on Colin's cheek, and he seemed to calm down instantly.

"Matri," he said, and leaned his head into her caressing touch.

A bolt of jealousy shot unexpectedly through Mia, but Domini put a hand on her arm when she would have stepped forward.

"It's okay," Domini whispered. "She's Anjelica, the head of his clan. His great-aunt, I think."

"She doesn't look like anybody's great-aunt," Mia whispered back.

"You flatter me, Prime's Chosen," Anjelica said, turning to Mia. The older woman smiled and held a hand out toward her. "We've had enough of wrangling and explanations. You've been through enough. I came here to celebrate the happy occasion of a bonding ceremony. I think we'll have the ceremony this evening." She shot a stern look at Colin. "Don't you agree, Reynard Prime?"

Colin didn't even look at Mia. He bowed his head and looked up at Anjelica from under his heavy dark brows. Mia saw that his gaze was defiant, and felt his seething anger—anger he directed at her.

But his voice was totally neutral when he spoke to the other woman. "Tonight, Matri. As you desire."

Chapter Thirteen

"Look what we caught."

"Caught him sneaking outside the house."

"He didn't put up much of a fight."

Laurent kept silent and didn't offer any resistance as the trio of Manticore Primes manhandled him into the room and shoved him to his knees before the pack leader.

"So you've come back," Justinian said, stepping up and slapping Laurent's already bloody face.

"We thought he'd run for good," one of the Primes who'd caught him said.

Justinian sent a look around the room that reined all his pack into silence. Even though the lesser Primes backed off, Laurent was all too aware of the malevolent attention focused on him. They were hungry for any excuse to vent aggression, and right now he appeared easy prey to them.

Laurent focused his attention on the truly dangerous one in the room. He made himself look at Justinian, and smile. And rise slowly to his feet.

Justinian let him do these things without striking him again. "Well?" he demanded. "Why did you desert the pack two nights ago? Why have you come back? Why were you skulking around my lair?" He sent a hard look to his beta Prime. "Did he betray us to the Clans? Have they hunted us to this lair?"

"No, Justinian," Belisarius answered promptly. "We made a careful search of the area. There are guards on watch." He gestured toward Laurent. "He is the only—"

"Do you want me to answer your questions or not?" Laurent interrupted, annoyed at having lost Justinian's attention. The night wasn't getting any younger.

And why were Tribe Manticore too damned old-fashioned to use the drugs that gave the Clans and Families the advantage of living twenty-four/seven, instead of creeping around in the dark like a bunch of movie vampires? Oh yeah, the Clan wouldn't let them.

He pushed that frustrating question out of the way, and went on. "I didn't desert the fight in the garage, I escaped a Clan attack—just like your boys did. The point of the exercise is to keep the

Clans off our asses. When your loyal minions ran back here—where the Clan might have been able to follow—I went looking for information. That was why you brought me in on this operation, right? To find the woman without the Clans getting wind of a tribe in their territory?"

"Not that you've managed to keep our presence secret," Belisarius accused.

"The Clans have no right to dictate where and what we hunt," Justinian proclaimed angrily. Then he shrugged, acknowledging the reality of the situation. "Yet they do. I didn't come to Los Angeles to start a war, but to get what is mine back."

"Hold that thought," Laurent said. "Because I think that's a strategy that might come in handy."

Justinian gave him a fiercely stern look. "Go on."

"I wasn't skulking around," Laurent went on. "I returned only after I had something useful to offer you, and was I scouting out the property to make sure neither Clan nor human hunter had found the lair when your boys jumped me."

"Hunters!" Justinian shouted. He spat on his fancy carpet. Then he swore in a harsh and ancient language. "How I loathe those murdering, thieving mortal pests. At least fighting vampire-to-vampire has some honor in it, some challenge. But being forced to fight mortals—"

His lips drew back in a vicious, fanged snarl.

"It's a dirty job, but somebody has to do it," Laurent muttered under his breath.

"What?"

"Nothing. Can I go on now?"

"You may." Justinian regally granted his permission.

"I keep a low profile in this town," Laurent said, "but I'm the most well-informed vampire in Los Angeles. I've spent the last couple of nights finding out what the Clan wants with the woman, and with us, now that they know I'm not the only Manticore in town."

"How dare you call yourself Manticore?" Belisarius demanded.

His comment was followed by angry snarls from others in the pack, but Justinian held up a silencing hand.

"And what did you find out, might-be Manticore?"

"Wannabe," someone muttered.

Laurent reined in his Prime reaction to start a brawl. He was already restraining the urge to taunt them that it had taken three of them to subdue him when he'd actually been *trying* to get inside.

"What I found out is that the Garrison woman had been the plaything of a Reynard

Prime, but he'd moved on before we found her. His interest was in her hot little body and a psychic edge she brought to the sex."

"Sounds like you're going to enjoy more than just torturing her," Belisarius said to Justinian.

The pack leader nodded before looking back at Laurent. "You're saying this Clan maggot had no idea who she is?" Justinian demanded suspiciously.

Laurent nodded. "For him she was a bed toy he met during some heroic rescue, I hear. I don't think they talked much."

"Why talk to a woman? And a mortal at that," Belisarius spoke up.

The other lesser Primes laughed. Laurent and Justinian ignored this byplay.

"Then why was the Clan male there when I sent you for the woman?"

"A blood call, is my guess. I think he drank a little too deep, and the craving hadn't worn off yet. He was trying *not* to return to her, in typically noble Clan fashion. So he was hanging around moping, and got in my way instead." Laurent snorted in disgust. "He assumed I wanted her for myself because he'd had her first, which was better than guessing the truth. But now all the Clan allies have closed ranks to protect the woman. They've taken her to the Shagal citadel."

Justinian hissed, and looked around at his small Manticore pack. "How am I to get my prey out of such a guarded place?" He glared at Laurent. "How are *you*?"

"I have more news, before I get to that."

"More? Worse, you mean."

"Another complication, at least. It seems that the Clans are on one of their noble quests to root evil out of the world. They're looking for some mortal bad guy who calls himself the Patron. Sounds sort of like a Tribe title, doesn't it?"

"The Patron, eh?" Justinian chuckled. "Do they know about Garrison?"

"Not yet. We have the advantage there, and I think we're going to have to use it. You see, the Clans are planning on turning the information about our being in town over to the vampire hunters."

Justinian drew himself up in outrage. "They'd deal with humans against their own kind?"

Yeah, well, boss, the times they are a changin'. "My sources tell me that old Tony Crowe had an appointment to talk to the hunter leader yesterday, but events at the Shagal place prevented him from keeping it," Laurent said.

"What events?"

"I haven't a clue, but every Clan member in town is gathered there. And some flew in from

Idaho. I'm guessing your prey is involved. No doubt Tony plans to reschedule the meeting. That'll leave the woman with the Clans, and the hunters on our tails. We need to act fast."

"What would you have us do?" Belisarius demanded. "Raid the Citadel? Battle the humans? Run?"

Running would have been Laurent's first choice, except for the promised payday. He kept his attention on Justinian. "I do have a suggestion."

It involved using brains rather than fangs, so there was no guarantee this lot would go along. But the only one who had to was the pack leader. The others would obey without question. Such blind obedience had never made much sense to Laurent. Right now, he wondered why he was tempted to reclaim any place in the Tribe. Maybe when this was over, and he was rich, he'd reevaluate his social ambitions.

Justinian considered him in silence, and tension grew in the room. The other Primes were not at all happy that the pack leader had brought Laurent into their midst. They itched for any excuse to fall on him and tear him to pieces. If Justinian repudiated him now, there was going to be a lot of bloodshed here tonight—though Laurent was the only one who wasn't certain most of the blood was going to be his. He felt mental probes from the others, telepathic taunts and threats, and ignored them. It was the silent, unmoving Justinian he concentrated on.

After a long time, just when Laurent could feel the boys getting ready to pounce, Justinian finally spoke.

"All right: what do you suggest I do?"

"As you desire." Mia paced back and forth in the bedroom, muttering furiously as she walked. "What did he mean, *as you desire*? Who the hell is that woman? What does she mean by bonding ceremony? Who is she to give orders? Since when does Colin Foxe take orders from anybody?"

"He takes orders from his matri," Domini answered.

Mia spun around on the deep plush carpet to face the vampire woman. Domini was seated on one of the chairs near the bookcase, her legs drawn up, looking calm and ever so slightly amused. She'd accompanied Mia back to the bedroom— apparently to wait with her while some sort of wedding ceremony was being cobbled together.

"I've been through this," Domini had said when they'd come in. "I can help."

Mia had ignored the offer in favor of angry pacing. She'd been so intent on fuming that she'd forgotten Domini's presence until now.

"And only *his* matri, at that," Domini went on. "Colin's a stubborn one. That's one of the reasons Serisa sent for Anjelica. She knew he's in too crazy a state right now to answer to anyone but the head of his clan. When a matri gives an order, Primes obey. They're matriarchal, and the only thing that keeps those big, bad boys in line is a strict code of honor and respect for women." She grinned conspiratorially at Mia. "And we women must only use our powers for good."

Mia digested what Domini told her, and ventured, "So Anjelica rules the—Primes—of Colin's clan."

Domini nodded. "That would be Clan Reynard. Serisa is head of Clan Shagal. Clans contain houses, and each house is headed by a daughter, aunt, sister, or female cousin of the matri. So a Prime, say my Alec, would introduce himself as Alexander Reynard, House Anjelica, Clan Reynard. It's complicated, like any culture. It has a certain old-fashioned charm, but somebody really ought to write a manual for new vampire inductees."

"Joss Whedon, maybe," Mia suggested.

Domini laughed, then grew serious. "Advice: no pop culture vampire jokes around the older generations. They rarely get it, and if they do get it, they think it's disrespectful."

Mia filed this tidbit away. At least someone was finally telling her something about vampires, even if it was a vampire. "Okay. How do I tell the older generations from the younger, when they're all immortal?"

"Hardly immortal, just long-lived, and that's a good question. You just *know* after a while. It's not polite to ask a vampire's age, but speech patterns and personal style give clues. When I first met my grandmother, she was wearing a lace bustier instead of a leather one, and that's how I could tell the difference, even though she looked about twenty-five."

"I don't plan to be around long enough to tell."

Domini's expression was sympathetic, but slightly impatient. "Get over it, Mia," she advised. "Bonding is always meant to be. Nobody asks for it. You belong in Colin's world now."

"You mean I belong *to* Colin." Fury bubbled in Mia. "Maybe you don't see anything wrong with a mortal being some sort of blood slave to a vampire, but the mortal isn't happy about it."

"Blood slave?" Domini asked. "That's a Tribe term. How do you know about the Tribes?"

"My family are vampire hunters," Mia blurted out, and lifted her head proudly. "The Garrisons." If they could have their clans and houses and whatnot, she had an ancient ancestry, as well. "I'm from an old line of vampire hunters."

"Really? Me, too."

"I thought you were a vampire."

"My grandmother's a vampire, but my . . . Wait a minute, does Colin know about your affiliation? You haven't killed any—"

"No. No one in my family's hunted in generations. I only vaguely knew that vampires existed, before the blond one attacked me."

Domini twined a strand of long, dark hair around her finger and looked thoughtful for a moment. "This should be between you and Colin, and you'd better tell him soon."

"Why? Will the shock be too much for him? He's already ashamed enough to be involved with a mortal."

Domini shook her head. "It's hard on both of you that the matris decided to make your situation so public, but they were worried that he'd broken some very strict laws about bonding. They felt it was necessary to confront him like that, since he's young, stubborn, and more headstrong than most Primes."

"Oh, that's a joy to hear."

"If they'd thought for a moment that he'd forced you—"

"He didn't."

"See, you care for him. Or you wouldn't be so quick to defend him."

"He doesn't want *me*. And I don't want him . . . to be a vampire." Mia sighed dramatically. "But I suppose it's too late, on all counts."

"That's the spirit," Domini said with false cheer. Growing serious, she added, "Remember that he belongs to *you*, too. Don't let him get away with any shit."

Mia couldn't help but smile. "You sound like my friend Courtney. Oh, my God! Courtney!"

Domini jumped up from the chair. "What's wrong?"

"Courtney's going to kill me!"

Domini's hands landed on her shoulders. "Where? How?"

Mia realized that the woman was taking her literally. "Sorry. I—Courtney's my best friend. We've known each other forever, and we promised to be each other's maid of honor. And I don't want to marry Colin, I mean, not like— But since I have to, well, I just can't get married without Courtney being there! I mean, I don't want to have a wedding ceremony without having any say in the arrangements. Which sounds totally hysterical," she added.

"Yeah."

Mia felt unaccustomed tears well up. Not

only was it impossible to contact her best friend, but it certainly wouldn't be right to bring Courtney into a lair of vampires. And it hurt terribly to be cut off from her friend. From her family. She had no friends here, no one she could really believe and trust. Not even Colin, who so clearly didn't want a human mate.

"So much for my special day," she murmured, and turned away from the other woman.

She took a deep breath. Domini was right: she needed to get over it, get on with it, and figure what to do with what she had to work with. Maybe she could come up with some way of escaping during this blood bond ceremony, or at the reception.

Mia began to laugh as she wondered what sort of wedding reception vampires held. Domini looked at her, but there was a knock on the door before she could say anything.

The door opened, and Alec stepped inside. "We have a new wrinkle in the situation. The ceremony might be a little later than we planned." He gave Mia an uncomfortable glance.

"What did Colin do?" she asked.

"He just smashed Tony over the head and fled the Citadel. It looks like we're going to have a search party instead of a bachelor party."

Chapter Fourteen

$\mathcal{M}$ia was aware that someone spoke to her, that someone touched her shoulder, but it didn't matter. There was a landscape painting on one wall of the bedroom. It looked like maybe it was a view of the Italian countryside, a warm, sunny place far, far from here. Mia stared at it and wished herself away.

"Anywhere but here," she murmured

He didn't want anything to do with her. He'd abandoned her. Left her in a den of vampires. Even if he was a vampire too, at least he was her—

"Mia. Mia, focus."

The voice belonged to Alec. The tone was one that expected to be obeyed. Mia ignored him.

"Mia, where is he?" Domini asked gently.

This got her attention, and Mia finally turned back to the couple. "Gone," she said, looking at Alec. "You said he was gone."

"But where is he?" Alec asked. "It would help if you told us."

"What's he talking about?" Mia asked Domini.

"You're bonded to him," Alec said impatiently.

Domini put a hand on his shoulder. "She really doesn't comprehend what it means yet. You are psychically linked to Colin," Domini told her. "*You're* psychic."

"No, I'm not." She remembered sharing thoughts with Colin. She knew that kind of communication came from both of them and wasn't just because he was a vampire. "Unless— Is being able to share thoughts with one person psychic?"

"It's a beginning," Domini said. "Your talent must be latent. Mortals tend to put up natural barriers to their own gifts, but one day your full potential will just explode. It'll develop as your relationship with Colin grows."

"But right now we need to find Colin," Alec insisted.

"What relationship? Hell, if the man wants to go, let him. Leave him alone. And I don't want to be here, either," she reminded the vampire couple.

"You can't be left alone. The matris have declared—"

"I don't answer to yo' mama!"

Alec's mouth hung open in shock for a moment.

Domini put a hand over her mouth, but her eyes sparkled with laughter. "Twenty-first century, my darlin' bondmate," she said when she had her amusement under control. "Young people these days, and all that."

Alec shook his head. "Mia, we of the Clans are a civilization with ancient laws and strict codes of conduct. Colin has agreed to the bonding ceremony. For him to go back on his word given to his Clan Matri is punishable by death. Twenty-first century or not, Colin's life is forfeit if he breaks his word."

Mia gasped, and this time she couldn't stop the tears, or from shaking as sobs wracked her.

"What's the matter?" she heard Alec ask. "Ow! What?"

"You just told a woman that a man would rather die than marry her," Domini said.

"I didn't say that! Besides, he can't *not want* to marry her. There must be something else going on."

"Tony's convinced that unconsciously bonding has made Colin unstable."

"Tony is currently unconscious. And when he wakes up, everyone in the Citadel is going to know that Colin's gone. Then Serisa and Mother are going to hit the roof, and the shi—"

"You mean you haven't told anyone else yet?" Domini asked.

"He managed to get out without anyone but me noticing. That's why I need your help, Mia. You, Domini, and I can leave the Citadel to find him."

"Shopping," Domini suggested. "They'll understand Mia wanting a dress for tonight."

"Once away from the Citadel, Mia can lead us to Colin, then we can bring them back here."

"Or we could leave them alone to work through their problems," Domini suggested.

"It can't happen that way," Alec answered.

Mia registered Alec's sounding all adamant and stern, and Domini's pragmatism, and she almost laughed. As insane as this situation was, the couple sounded so normal in the way they dealt with each other. Then it registered with her that Alec thought Colin was behaving this way because he was sick. Guilt and concern overrode the tearing pain of abandonment.

"Did I make him sick?" she asked, turning back to them. *Or is he just a jerk?*

Either way, he was still a vampire. Why did she keep forgetting the intrinsic evil of these people? Probably because she had Colin's blood flowing through her veins.

Abomination. The ugly word swam up from the few things she'd learned from her grandmother. It was the term vampire hunters used for those who consorted with the enemy.

She pulled herself together. She wanted to get away and they were offering her a way out. Once she was away from the Citadel with only these two guarding her, she'd be able to find a way to escape.

"I'll help you find Colin," she told them. "Let's hurry."

Colin stood in the shadow of the low stucco building and waited while the woman crossed the small parking lot. He didn't know where she lived, but he knew where she worked, so this was where he'd come to find her. It wouldn't have been prudent to barge in and grab her, so he stood outside and telepathically called until she came outside.

If he'd had his cellular phone with him this would have been easier, but his fellow clansmen had deprived him of his modern possessions.

The young woman he wanted was slender, long-legged and blond, young and attractive, and wearing a short blue print dress that showed off all her best assets. She wasn't his favorite person in the world, even though he appreciated looking at her. In fact, he considered her an inconvenience, but it wasn't as if he'd made an effort to get to know her. Right now she was important to him.

He waited until she was at her car before he made his move. He was standing behind her before she could open the car door. When he touched her shoulder, she jumped and turned, and her eyes went wide in surprise.

"What the hell are *you* doing here?"

He smiled, cocking his head to one side. "I came for you."

She frowned at him and started to protest.

But Colin looked into her eyes and slipped past her weak mental barriers with ease. *I can explain everything. And you're going to love this.*

"What the *hell* does he think he's doing?"

The sudden jab of possessive anger that went through Mia caused as much physical pain as mental pain. Enough to make her screw her eyes shut—which only gave her a disturbingly vivid image of the couple standing next to a red car. She knew the car, and the woman.

"What's he doing with her?"

Mia's head hurt so much she was barely aware of Domini sitting beside her in the backseat.

"Colin?" Domini asked.

Alec stopped the car so quickly she was thrown forward against the seatbelt. The jolt broke her concentration, but not so much that she wasn't *aware* of the connection linking her to—

"That cheating son of a—"

"Colin," Alec said.

Mia looked at Domini. "I've felt when he was with other women before, and told myself it was imagination. But I just *saw* him."

Domini nodded encouragingly. "The more blood you share, the closer you become."

They were surrounded by heavy traffic on the busy street. Many car horns sounded, and Alec responded by driving slowly on. "Where is he?" he asked Mia. "Which way do I go?"

Mia put her head back against the seat's plush headrest and closed her eyes once more. The air conditioner hummed, and cool air slid over her skin. Domini's hand was warm on her arm. All these sensations were easy to block out. When she let herself concentrate on it, she became exquisitely *aware* of where Colin was.

She'd been fighting the hunger to be with Colin for months. In fact, the struggle not to find him had become a habit, one that had driven her nearly crazy.

It was time for her to give up the fight. The vampires wanted to find Colin. And she *needed* to.

And when she did, all her instincts urged her to whomp his ass for daring to be with another woman.

"Left," she told Alec. "Left at the next street."

"Sweet," Colin said.

He was speaking of the maneuver the black SUV's driver had used to force him to pull the red sports car over to the curb and block it from pulling out again. He might have been concerned if he hadn't recognized the vehicle, or been aware that Mia was one of the passengers.

As it was, he acceded to the situation and said to the woman beside him, "This is fun."

While she wasn't completely in his thrall, he exerted enough influence over her to keep her calm. He got out of the car, and the woman followed him. Mia jumped out of the back of the SUV and rushed toward him. He recognized the look in her eyes, having felt the same way when she was with Tony.

"What the hell do you think you're doing with my best friend?"

"Hi, Mia," Courtney said, coming up beside him.

Mia lunged.

Colin caught Mia in his arms before she could do any damage to anyone.

"Sweetheart, I know exactly how you feel," he told her.

Then he kissed her, and the usual fire threatened to explode between them. Damn, he loved kissing her!

She resisted for a moment, which only made him more urgent. Then Mia ground her body against his, and Colin forgot everything but the urge to lay her down on the hood of the car. Her nails pressed hard against his shoulders told him she wouldn't mind.

"You're holding up traffic, officer."

Colin heard Alec's comment as though from a great distance, but awareness of the other Prime helped him to reluctantly break the kiss. For a moment he saw only red, and all he could breathe was Mia's scent. They were standing in the street with cars flashing past inches away. He moved onto the sidewalk, where the others joined them.

Then Mia moved away from him, and he was able to get himself fully under control.

She looked from him to her friend. "Courtney, what are you doing with Colin?"

There was still an edge of jealousy in her

voice, and Colin couldn't help but smile at this proof that she wanted him. "I felt your need to be with your friend so strongly, I had to do something."

"That was a bit impulsive," Alec said.

Colin concentrated on Mia. "So I was bringing her to you to be a bridesmaid. I wanted to do something nice for you."

"Aw . . . ," Domini said.

He ignored the sarcasm. Mia was all that mattered. She was looking at him not just with confusion, but with a certain amount of cautious hope. She touched his cheek, and the connection was as electric as ever.

"You kidnapped Courtney? For me?" She sounded unwillingly pleased.

Courtney laughed. "He asked nicely." She gave Colin a wry look. "Which I didn't expect from him, but I have to admit, I'm beginning to understand what you see in him."

"Did you hypnotize her?" Mia asked him.

"I used charm," he answered.

"So of course I said I'd come with him," Courtney went on. "Especially after he told me how the two of you had been in intensive couple's counseling for the last week. I was wondering why you weren't answering my calls. I was worried, girl, and I think this quickie wedding idea is a little on the impulsive side, but if that's what you want, you know I'm here for you, like I always am." Courtney took a deep breath, and added, "Do you even have a dress yet?"

"That's exactly where we were heading when we ran into you," Domini said. Colin was relieved when she stepped in to take charge. "Why don't you two head back to Serisa's," she told him and Alec, "while the three of us head over to Rodeo Drive. Don't worry," she added to Alec's dubious look. "I'll be sure to have them back in time for the party."

Chapter Fifteen

"When I was born," Serisa said, "the world was still lit by candles, by fires, and gaslights and oil lamps. And we have always walked by moonlight and starlight, which are the reflections of distant fire. We saw the world by fire, and fire has always burned in us. In this age we live by both sun and candlelight, but the quest to find our bondmates has not changed. Two here have fulfilled that quest. We of the Clans come together to witness the binding of Two Who Burn as One."

Serisa stood on the edge of a wide terrace, her back to a garden fragrant with roses and jasmine. The terrace was lit by hundreds of white candles, and filled with arrangements of red and white flowers in crystal vases. Overhead the moon shone as a silver crescent, and stars were visible despite the lights of the city. Anjelica and Barak stood to the Shagal Matri's right and left, and a small table was in front of them.

All the other vampires were gathered on the terrace, as well. They applauded her words and spoke their approval.

"When two fires join to blend into a greater flame, that is when we know our greatest joy."

There were more murmurs of agreement.

Mia stood on the other side of the terrace in her orchid gown and looked around in shocked wonder at the proceedings. She carried a bouquet of orchids as well, and one was tucked into her short brown curls. She felt beautiful, even though butterflies fluttered in her stomach.

She was as nervous as any bride, she supposed.

While a part of her tried to remind her that she was caught up in a monster movie nightmare, she couldn't listen to that part of herself right now. She was touched, genuinely touched and pleased at the beauty and goodwill that surrounded her. They had done this for her. Best of all, Colin had—

"Ready to rock?" Courtney whispered.

—brought her friend to be with her. She'd been promised that Courtney would be taken safely home afterward, with only pleasant memories of the event. *And no bite marks,* Tony had said. *I promise.*

Mia smiled at Courtney, then at Domini, who was also standing with her.

"You look beautiful," Domini told her.

"Thank you."

It was Lady Anjelica who had found Mia's dress. Anjelica and Serisa showed up at the exclusive dress shop only moments after Domini had ushered her and Courtney inside—a subtle reminder that Mia was a prisoner. There'd been no chance to escape, but the shopping had been glorious. The dress finally chosen was long and slinky; the bias cut gave the dress an elegant but sexy 1930s look. It made Mia feel rather like Jean Harlow.

Maybe she wasn't draped in virginal bridal white, but this was hardly a traditional marriage. "I guess *until death do you part* takes on new meaning when your're dealing with vampires," Mia whispered.

Domini nodded.

"What?" Courtney asked.

On the other side of the terrace, Serisa raised her hands and said, "Let the Bonded be brought together."

"You know, you didn't have to hit me," Tony said.

He was standing to Colin's left while they

waited in the garden. Colin didn't glance his way; his attention was focused on the brightness on the terrace above.

"Yeah, but it was fun," he answered.

"You should thank Tony, instead of taking your resentment out on him," Alec said from his other side.

Though he would have preferred to have his own friends or his brother standing witness with him, Colin was grateful enough that his cousin and the Corvus Prime were with him. But he didn't want to hear their advice on women, even if this was the traditional time to offer it.

"Of course, if your friends were standing here," Tony picked up Colin's thoughts, "they'd be ragging you about settling for a mortal."

"And then you'd have to beat the crap out of them," Alec added.

Would I? Colin wondered. He would, because his bondmate's honor was his honor, and a Prime's honor was everything. "I'm more old-fashioned than I thought."

"Good thing, too," Alec answered. "It means you'll do right by that girl, whether you want to or not."

"I'll take care of her."

"Like a person, not a pet," Tony insisted.

As Serisa said, "Let the Bonded be brought

together," Colin took a sharp breath, all the dread of this moment suddenly forgotten. Mia was up there.

He moved across the garden and up the marble stairs with swift urgency. He vaguely recalled that Alec had told him this part of the ceremony symbolized climbing from dark into light as he reached the candlelit terrace. But symbolism didn't matter, as long as Mia was up there waiting for him.

"You are so beautiful," Colin said as he and Mia met.

She was more beautiful than he remembered, even though he'd only seen her a few hours ago. Why hadn't he really noticed how beautiful she was before?

He reached for her. She swiftly gave her bouquet to Courtney and took his hands. He wanted to say more, but neither thoughts nor words would come, only emotions. He was so good at erecting psychic barriers, at compartmentalizing his feelings, but suddenly he had no barriers at all.

What good were barriers when they kept him apart from Mia?

She looked into his eyes, which were aglow with hope. She smiled. It was shy, tentative, but it set him on fire.

Colin drew Mia into his arms. Their bodies came together, and their lips touched. For that instant everything became clear, and he became whole. They became whole.

As if from a great distance he heard Lady Serisa say, "The Blessing of Fire is granted to Reynard Prime Colin and his lady Caramia."

Caramia. Mia. *His* Mia. What a beautiful name, Caramia. As lovely as any vampire name.

Caramia, he whispered into her mind. *Caramia mine.*

Colin, she answered.

The next thing Mia knew, they were facing Barak and the matris across the width of the silk-draped table. Courtney and Domini were standing on her other side; Alec and Tony flanked Colin. A gold cup was placed at the center of the table. It looked heavy and ancient, and was decorated with Egyptian symbols and filled with red liquid.

For the first time Mia felt a moment of panic. Was she going to have to drink *blood*? In public?

Barak leaned forward and whispered, "It's all right. It's a sort of cinnamon drink; cold and hot, sweet and fiery, all at once."

"Kind of like magic Moutain Dew," Colin added.

Mia stifled a giggle as Serisa gave them a stern

look. The Matri was obviously not going to allow any levity to mar this grave and solemn occasion.

Serisa reached out. "Give me your left hand," she directed Colin. "Your right," she told Mia. She entwined her fingers with theirs over the cup.

Mia and Colin were already holding hands, and energy poured through her and from her, making her part of a psychic circle. When Serisa spoke again, it was directly into her and Colin's minds.

Your yearning souls sought and found each other all uncaring of your conscious wills. Your minds must bend to the will of your joined souls. You fight the inevitable to your cost. To wound each other is to wound yourselves. Bend or break, but the bond will remain. Live in joy at what you have found, for the true and complete soul bonding is rare among vampire and mortal kind. Those who seek it do not always find it. You have not sought it, yet the treasure is yours. Guard it, nurture it. Guard and nurture each other.

"I will," Mia said, though she hadn't meant to speak.

After a hesitation, Colin also said, "I will."

Then Serisa placed their hands on either side of the gold cup. "Witness," she said to the others.

Alec, Tony, Courtney, and Domini all gravely responded, "I witness."

The metal beneath Mia's fingers suddenly began to grow warm. Then the liquid within the cup began to glow. She almost didn't believe what she was seeing, but she was completely fascinated.

Are we doing that? she asked Colin as the light continued to grow.

Yeah. He was as awed as she was.

The light and warmth spread into her, through her, through Colin, and back to her. This was magic, true magic, true completion.

When the moment was right, and they somehow *knew* it was right, they gently lifted the cup. Colin held it to Mia's lips for the first sip. She held a few drops on her tongue while she held the cup to Colin's lips, then Alec took the cup from them. She closed her eyes and let this magical potion take her.

It tasted exactly as Barak had described, and more. It tasted like the essence of love.

"Your souls merge, your blood entwines, forever claiming what you are to each other." Anjelica spoke for the first time. "Colin Foxe, Prime of House Athena of Clan Reynard, your Matri recognizes the undeniable truth of your Bonding. Caramia Luchese, mortal daughter of Catherine, your Clan welcomes a new daughter into our keeping. Kiss now, and let the Binding be sealed."

Colin took her in his arms, and when their lips met, she forgot everyone and everything but Colin, and that he tasted of love.

"Great party," Colin said to her, after one more Prime finished giving good wishes and advice and moved away.

Mia was well aware that her "bondmate" was getting tired of all the attention, but they'd been told it was their duty to stand here by the terrace steps and speak to the guests. Mia was still too full of excitement at finally learning about vampires to be bored. For example, she found it interesting that instead of a reception line, the vampires solemnly came up one by one for private conversations.

"Great party, indeed," she replied, gazing around at groups of people who were laughing and flirting with each other.

Couples kept disappearing down the garden stairs and into the house. There was a joyous air of sexual tension in the atmosphere. It was pretty obvious that people got laid a lot at vampire parties. These were highly sensual, sexual beings, and quite comfortable with it.

"Maybe we should dance or something," she

suggested to Colin, relishing the idea of moving slowly with her body pressed against his. "The bride and groom can do that, right? It's a way for us to be left alone for a while."

A group of guests were playing classical music on one side of the terrace; the vampire musicians were very talented. She supposed that they had plenty of time to develop their skill.

"They're playing a waltz," Colin said. "Do you know how to waltz?"

"No."

"Me, either. And we don't use terms like *bride* and *groom*," he explained. "Not for a bonding ceremony. We're mates, bondmates, bonded, but it's hard to translate into mortal terms. It's not gender-specific like husband and wife. It goes deeper than that."

She caught his sense of profound surprise that they shared this special vampire thing, and she nodded. "Me, too."

"We can't fight it," he said, responding to her understanding of him.

But did that mean that he wanted to fight it? Did she? Should they? Not right now; she was having too good a time. "Are you having a good time?"

He kissed her cheek. "Like I said, it's a great party."

Mia took another sip from a crystal flute and sighed. "This is the best champagne I've ever had."

"I'll get you another glass," Colin offered.

She put her hand on his sleeve when he turned toward the buffet table. "You know I never let myself have more than one glass of wine at a party."

He was still for a moment, then turned back to her with a puzzled look. "I do?" She nodded. He frowned. "I guess we don't know each other very well yet."

She settled her arm more snugly around his waist, leaning against him. Desire buzzed through her as it always did when he was near, and there was no frantic edge to it, no darker undercurrents. She was enjoying him, enjoying being with him, loving the anticipation of making love to him.

"This feels good," she said.

"You smell good," he answered.

"It's the perfume. Turns out Serisa uses the same brand my grandmother did. When she spritzed it on me, all these childhood memories came flooding back. It was kind of like having her with me—though I doubt she would have approved of you."

He laughed. "What sane granny would?"

"What about your family?" she asked. "I

know that Alec's a cousin, and that Anjelica's a great-aunt, right?"

"Right."

"What about the rest of your family? Will they approve of me? Do you wish they were here?"

"We'll have another ceremony for your family," he said. "A mortal-style wedding."

He had evaded her question. "Will your mom and granny and brothers and sisters come?"

"I don't have a sister, but my mother and brother will welcome you into the Clan. Both my grandmothers are dead," he added. "And don't say you're sorry, because Grandmother Genevieve was nearly six hundred years old when she passed away. Even for a vampire, that's ancient."

Mia's mind boggled at this information. And it reminded her that her great-grandfather—who was ancient by mortal standards—had talked a lot about how wrong it was for something as monstrous as vampires to hold the secret to eternal life. It seemed that they weren't exactly immortal, but . . .

"Six hundred. Whoa. That's impressive."

"So was she. I'm told she was a tough old matri, but the old lady I remember was sweet, and loved to spoil kids."

Mia wondered just how vampires spoiled their children—and about vampire children, and about having vampire children.

"What about your other grandmother?" she asked, grasping for a focus before her mind completely boggled.

Anger and pain clouded Colin's expression. Mia didn't think he was going to answer, but after a moment he said, "I never knew Grandmother Antonia, my father's mother. She was captured by one of the tribes long before I was born. Those are the bad-guy vampires out of mortal legend," he told her. "They're as much our enemies as they are yours. They take our women when they can, as they did my grandmother. Like they tried to take you." His hold on her became suddenly tighter, more possessive and protective.

The tense moment was interrupted by the approach of another Prime. Mia hadn't yet seen a vampire who wasn't spectacularly handsome or beautiful, but this blond male also had an aura of sorrow and weariness about him that was almost palpable.

His smile was still charming, though, and there was a hint of goodwill in his hazel eyes when he looked at her. "I wish you joy, lady of Reynard. And you," he added, looking to Colin,

"I wish you all the time in the world to enjoy what you have. Cherish each day." Then he kissed Mia's hand and walked away.

Colin looked after him with the sort of awe Mia had never expected to see from her cocky SWAT cop. "I didn't think he'd be here," he murmured.

"Who is he?"

"David Berus, Clan Serpentes. The Viper himself."

"And that translates to a language I understand as . . . ?"

"Bravest of the Brave, the most primal of the Primes. And the only one who's ever survived losing a bondmate. It drove him crazy for about fifty years. I hear that's why he volunteered to be the guinea pig when they first developed the daylight drugs. He didn't have anything to lose, so he let the scientists experiment on him. He was the first to walk in daylight—though I don't suppose seeing the sun made up for what he lost."

Music still floated across the terrace, the tune melancholy. It added to Mia's sense of sadness over what Colin told her about the other Prime's loss. "How did he lose her?" she asked. "I thought bonding was forever." To lose forever would be awful.

"A band of Purists murdered her," Colin answered. "The evil fanatics cut off her head. David was on the other side of the world when it happened, probably saving mortal lives. The mortal hunters don't care what kind of vampires they kill, as long as they kill vampires."

The hatred he projected frightened Mia. How was she supposed to explain that she had set out to be a vampire hunter herself?

Domini had advised her to tell Colin about her family soon, and it sounded like good advice. But it probably wasn't the best subject to bring up to a vampire husband on one's wedding night. That it felt so very right to be married to this vampire was confusing enough.

"You know," she said, with a shaky smile, "I think I will let you get me that second glass of champagne."

Chapter Sixteen

"Can you read my mind?"

Mia really meant, Can you reach deep into my thoughts and rip out anything you want to know about me? But this didn't seem like the time or place to ask such a blunt, frightening question.

Colin thought this was an odd question for Mia to ask, when they were finally alone. They'd just endured a ceremony that he found down-right medieval and silly. Everybody at the party had escorted them into Serisa's most luxurious guest room, where they'd been put into bed together. A shivaree? Or maybe the shivaree thing was the old bride-kidnapping custom. His memory of folklore was dim at the moment.

He guessed maybe Mia didn't want to talk about how strange the last few minutes had been, but it still seemed like an odd question. He studied her as she sat propped up against a pile of pale satin pillows, with a sheet drawn up to her bare shoulders and a pensive look on her lovely face.

"We've been sharing thoughts for months," he reminded her. "Mostly communicating without even knowing it."

"And you've been messing with my memories."

"For your own goo—" He stopped when she shook a finger at him, and made him laugh. Okay, it was time to stop being defensive. "I only touched the surface of your mind," he promised her. "I never consciously went deeper than that."

"But you could?"

Okay, a little paranoia on her part was understandable, but they had better things to do with the rest of the night than talk.

He began tugging slowly on the sheet covering her as he answered. "The kind of mind reading I think you're talking about is really very hard to do, at least if you don't want to leave your subject brain-damaged. I've heard that Tribe vampires mentally rape their victims—but we do *not* want to talk about that."

She shook her head. "Definitely not."

Mia was safe here, and was going to stay safely in the Shagal citadel until the Tribe vampires who'd hunted her were dealt with. Or maybe he'd take her to his own clan's stronghold in Idaho. But that would mean introducing her to the likes of Flare and Maja, the Clan daughters he'd been courting. Although he cared deeply for Mia, he wasn't ready to acknowledge that a Clan match was forever out of his reach.

Bend or break, Serisa had said. But he had to do this in his own time and way. He had no choice but to make the effort. And—

"Colin?"

He blinked, and looked at Mia. Without noticing it he'd pulled the sheet down around her waist, baring her lovely round breasts. The warm tint of her tanned skin contrasted beautifully against the pale satin. He pulled the sheet all the way off, taking in her sensually rounded hips and the firm curves of her legs.

She reached out and touched his cheek, and the contact sent blazing heat through him.

"Colin, are you with me?"

"Oh, yeah," he said, and bent his head to take a nipple in his mouth. He suckled, and teased it with his tongue and teeth when it grew stiff, loving the taste and texture. Mia's breasts were wonderful.

Her response was as quick as his need. She caressed his back and shoulders while he moved down her body, breathing in her warm female scent, tasting her skin with quick licks and kisses.

He was aroused by the sharp awareness of blood rushing beneath warm flesh. His fangs were extending quickly, and his cock was already hard. Flesh and blood both called to him, the need to possess both growing in him. He sensed and savored the way her body changed as she became more and more aroused.

Mia tried not to let herself go, not to lose herself instantly this time. But Colin's gentlest caress was explosive, making it almost impossible not to fall into sensory overload. She couldn't stay lucid for long when he touched her.

She was aware of the soft mattress beneath them, and of the smooth satin sheet and pillows at her back; the brush of cool air was a stark contrast to the heat of their naked skin. But most of her world was taken up by the feel of sinewy hard muscles beneath her hands, and the glory of Colin's clever mouth working wonders, moving from her breast to her stomach, and farther down. Every few moments the edge of a fang brushed across her skin. Anticipation of the sharp combination of pain and ecstasy set her senses reeling.

This searing expectation was familiar, but this was the first time she was actually fully aware of what was happening.

"And I like it."

Colin lifted his head. "What?"

She ran her fingers through his hair. "Don't ever stop."

Colin laughed, and she felt the sound against her skin. The same way she felt his pleasure at giving her pleasure. She closed her eyes and rode sensation while his head came between her spread thighs. His highly skilled tongue darted and licked across her slick, swollen flesh. She squirmed and moaned as lightning seared deep inside, where it coiled and grew, tighter and larger, and finally burst through her.

Colin cried out at her orgasm. His body arched away from hers, then he grabbed her by the waist and pulled her to him across the smooth satin sheet, and his cock entered her in one smooth, hard thrust. This set off another orgasm, and her reaction drove him crazy—which drove her wild.

As the feedback loop rolled through them, their bodies came together in hard, frantic thrusts, thrashing limbs, and breathless, frenzied kisses on salty hot skin.

Mia was blinded by the roaring rush of orgasm after orgasm, but it still wasn't enough. The craving grew even as he came inside her and his release flashed nova-hot through her. The taste of Colin's skin was delicious, but what was beneath the surface still called to her. There was no way to resist, and her teeth pressed into Colin's shoulder.

Her mouth filled with sweet copper fire, though there was only a drop or two on her tongue. Vampire blood was so sweet.

Colin pulled away with a hard, surprised jerk, and he was up off the bed an instant later. Mia watched him in a languorous fog, too heavy-limbed and brain-fogged with utter satisfaction to react to anything.

Colin, on the other hand, was full of furious energy. He grasped his shoulder and shouted, "You bit me!"

His glare could have ignited a wildfire, but Mia only smiled a little. "Uh-huh."

"You. Bit. Me." He spoke slowly and clearly, each word an accusation.

Mia languidly reach up and stroked the spot on her left breast where he had bitten her while they'd been making love. It was nice to remember him doing it, and how wonderful it had felt at the time. Though she wasn't quite sure when he had taken the quick nip that sent her into ecstasy. There'd been a lot of ecstasy in the last few minutes—hours?

She smiled as she continued to pet the healing mark. "That was nice."

Colin gazed at her breast and he felt himself growing hard again, just looking at Mia's naked body. His fangs ached to bury themselves in the exact spot she was so provocatively stroking. She was looking at him with a dazed, adoring, satiated expression that normally would have made him preen. Normally, he'd jump back into bed and start making love to her again.

But there was something very disturbing going on here, and he had to concentrate, hard as that was. As hard as *he* was.

"You *bit* me," he said for the third time.

"Yeah." Her eyes glittered with invitation, and she lifted a hand toward him. "Come here, and I'll do it again."

He curbed his natural impulses with some effort, and concentrated on justifiable anger. He had to turn his back on her. "You had no right to bite me."

"Why not? You bite me all the time."

He whirled back to her. "I'm a vampire! I'm supposed to bite you!"

"Is there something wrong with biting back?"

"Yes! You can't taste my blood without—"

"Your permission?" Irritation crept into her voice. "Why should I have to ask you for a bite, when you never asked me if it's okay?" She sensually stroked her breasts. "Which it is."

Her nipples were standing up, perky and demanding his attention. His body was growing tight with desire, but this had to be settled. "Because—"

"It works both ways, Colin."

"How long have you been biting me?"

She gave a slow, one-shoulder shrug. "I don't know. It just happens sometimes, when we get really wild. I don't usually remember doing it. Don't you remember getting bitten?"

"No."

"I didn't remember you biting me, either. So I guess that's fair."

"It's not fair. It's crazy. I deliberately made you forget when I tasted you."

"Well, maybe I made you forget."

"That's not possible!"

She gave another shrug, followed by a conciliatory smile. "Are we going to argue on our wedding night?"

"We are not married!" he shouted furiously, as a sense of betrayal took him. "We're bonded! We're stuck with each other forever!"

"Stuck?" Her voice sounded as sharp as broken glass.

"And it's your fault!"

Her hurt beat at him through his fury, through the ache of lust. For a moment, he hated himself for hurting her. He didn't mean it, not the way she thought he did. It was just—

Just that it wasn't supposed to happen this way!

He'd had his life planned out, knew all the right moves, the way a Prime's life was supposed to progress. It had all been going so fine until the night Mia Luchese kickboxed her way into his life.

Though that wasn't fair, and he knew it. He had pursued her, been determined to have her, the moment they met. But she was the one who caught him—and right now he hated the feeling. A few hours ago he'd made a vow to himself to accept his fate, to make the best of the situation.

Right now, all he wanted to do was walk out.

But she was hurting too, and she was his bondmate.

"Damn!" he snarled, and turned back to her.

Only for a knock to sound on the door before anything could be said or settled.

Chapter Seventeen

"Don't you dare open that door!" Mia demanded as Colin crossed the room. She was in no mood to be interrupted; no way was she going to let him get away with blaming her for all this. "Come back here and fight like a vampire!"

Colin snatched up her abandoned clothing as he passed the foot of the bed and tossed it to her. "Get dressed."

"Fuck you!"

"Don't tempt me."

His voice was cold, but the anger and implied threat radiating from him frightened Mia.

Colin didn't know who dared to interrupt them, but he was set to tear the intruder apart. He paused only long enough to make sure his bondmate's modesty was protected.

But when he reached the door, Colin leaned

his forehead against it for a moment. Despite the wild urges racing through him, a small, sane voice was trying to remind him that it was a Prime's duty to think before reacting. He was intensely aware of the smooth grain of the wood and the faded scent of the varnish. His sharp senses also detected both a male and a female waiting in the hallway. This gave his animal side some reassurance that the Prime on the other side of the door wasn't here to steal his mate.

The knock came again.

When he opened the door he found Barak and Serisa waiting in the hall. Barak was standing protectively in front of his bondmate, as though anticipating an attack.

Colin kept his hands at his sides, and his voice almost polite. "Yes?"

Serisa peered from behind her mate's wide shoulder and gave Colin's naked body a quick glance as she said, "We would not have interrupted you unnecessarily."

Colin accepted her once-over as his due. Bonded or not, young or old, a vampire had to be dead not to *look*. "Yes," he said again, his voice just barely calm enough not to give insult to the Matri.

"Your presence is required," Barak said. "Immediately."

Colin ran a hand across his face. His nerves were already frayed, but he knew they wouldn't have disturbed him if it wasn't important. SWAT call or Prime duty, he was used to having his private life disturbed.

Still, he couldn't help but say, "Why now?"

"We are sorry," Barak said. "But we have a situation with Tribe Manticore that concerns you and your lady."

"And requires your presence," Serisa added. "Both of you."

Mention of Tribe vampires redirected Colin's anger. He'd heard of the Manticores; real old-fashioned bad boys considered trash even by the low standards of the other tribes.

"I'm not letting my woman near a Manticore."

"It is required," Serisa said. "By the terms of the Understanding."

Colin frowned at the Matri. "Understanding? What are you talking about?" Suspicion gnawed at him. "Is this Understanding like a treaty? Do we have a treaty with the Tribes?" His voice rose in outrage at each question. "How come I've never heard of this?"

Barak put up a calming hand. "We have arrangements for parlays with the Tribes—a holdover from ancient times when the mortal hunters targeted all vampires. We do not stand with them, ever, but exchanges of information are sometimes necessary. The Manticore pack leader claims rights under the old ways."

"An *Understanding*," Colin scoffed.

"They approached our sentries just before dawn," Serisa told him. "They offered their vulnerability to sunlight as a show of good faith. They risked their lives for the chance to speak with us." She sighed. "I had no choice but to allowed them a daylight sanctuary, and parlay."

Colin thought she should have let these Manticores stand out in the sunlight and fry.

"For the parlay, Justinian of the Manticores says he requires your and Mia's presence," Serisa said.

"Please get dressed and come with us now," Barak said.

Colin was torn by several conflicting impulses. He was compelled to obey, because he'd been trained to obey the Matri and elders. He also wanted to tell them he wasn't letting Mia anywhere near the vampires that had attacked her, and slam the door in their faces.

He glanced over his shoulder to where Mia knelt in the center of the wide bed, wrapped in the cream-colored satin sheet. Her expression was one of curiosity, but her emotions still radiated anger and hurt. He felt them like a burning coal in his head, and in his soul.

He couldn't stand her pain.

"Your indulgence, Matri, Elder, but we can't join you right now." Colin took a step back, and began to slowly close the door on the surprised couple. "Tell the bottom-feeders we'll be there—when we're there," he finished as the door firmly shut.

He put everything going on outside this room out of his mind as he crossed the thick carpet to stand at the foot of the bed.

Mia watched his approach warily. "What do you want?"

"Let's talk," he said, holding up his hands before him. He took a deep breath, determined to stay calm. "Just talk. Okay?"

"Talk?"

She looked at him so suspiciously that he almost laughed. At least he felt her temper cooling down a little. That was his Mia: she flared white-hot at light speed, but she calmed down quickly enough. Her hurt wasn't going away, though.

He sat down on the end of the bed. "Come here."

When she didn't move, he grabbed her by the ankle and pulled her to sit beside him. He put his arm around her shoulder, partly to be comforting, partly to keep her from getting up and stalking away. She was stiff in his embrace for a moment, but soon relaxed against him. They couldn't help but want to touch each other. He waited in silence for her curiosity to build.

"What do you want to talk about?" she finally asked.

She looked up at him with those big brown eyes, and he wanted to do several things other than talk. Which would have been fine if she was just another mortal girl he desired.

"We don't have much time. Did you hear about the Tribe visitors?"

She scowled. "I heard. But—"

"When did you first bite me?" he interrupted. "Do you bite all your lovers?"

"All my lovers?" She laughed. "You're the only lover I've ever had."

"What?" His arm tightened around her. After a moment of shock, his memories rolled back to the first time they'd made love. All he remembered was passion—hot, hard, frantic, unbelievably mind-melting sex. He remembered the effects, but the details were vague. "Uh . . ." Colin swallowed hard. "Are you sure?"

He expected her to be offended, but she chuckled. "A woman generally remembers these things. You are the only lover I've ever had."

"But—it—you—we—"

"Fucked like bunnies. Or vampires, I guess."

"But you seemed so—involved. Shouldn't a virgin be more . . . virginal?"

She laughed again, obviously relishing his almost embarrassed confusion. "This isn't the Middle Ages. I read a lot of books with sex scenes, and saw a few R-rated movies before you came along—and I think instinct plays a part in knowing what to do."

"So—" He thought about it for a moment, then ventured, "When I bit you for the first time . . . you responded by . . . you followed my lead?"

She gave this some consideration. "Yeah. I guess that makes sense."

"So I'm your first, huh?" He pulled her even closer, her bare skin warm and soft against his side. "How about that." Too bad they didn't have a few more minutes.

"Oh, *please*," she complained. "Don't sound so smug, you slut."

"Guilty," he told her.

"And I knew every time you cheated on me. Did you know that?"

Colin started to say that he hadn't technically cheated on Mia, because since he had officially ended their relationship. But since they'd unknowingly fallen into the bonding process during the months they'd been lovers, and he suddenly felt the pain he left in her like deep, aching scars on his own soul, he understood her anger.

"It must have confused you," he said. "Knowing I was with other women, but not knowing how you knew."

"Did you know I was aware of you?"

"I tried not to think about you at all." She tried to draw away, but he wouldn't let her. "I know that's harsh, but it's true. I tried to forget you."

"Because I'm not a vampire."

"You were pretty upset to find out that I'm a vampire. You wouldn't have wanted me if you'd known the truth from the beginning."

"You can say that again," she muttered.

The comment hurt his pride, but Colin kept his hard-won calm. They didn't have the time to work out all their problems right now. "We have years—"

"That you'll be stuck with me," she interrupted.

"But I can't imagine being stuck with anyone else," he said. "Even when I was with other women, all I could see was you."

Mia gave him a furious look. "Oh, that really makes me feel good."

"Do you want me to say something sickeningly romantic?" She frowned, but shook her head. "I could say I wish all those nights in other women's beds hadn't happened. All I can say is that they *shouldn't* have happened, knowing what I know now. If I'd thought for a moment that we were bonding, I would have—"

What would he have done? Returned to Mia and begged her to take him back, instead of lingering near her and hating the need to be with her? If he'd suspected the start of a bond, he might have run off to his Clan citadel, seeking telepathic help, or to Dr. Casmerek's vampire clinic for some kind of scientific answer. But could they have helped? Would it have been right?

"My culture teaches that bonds are meant to be. Apparently the longer a Prime lives unbonded, the more he craves the bond and searches for his one true love. I'm still confused about what happened between us."

Mia was thoughtful for a moment. "If I hadn't bitten you and made you forget it, you probably wouldn't be in this mess."

"Don't apologize."

"I'm not. I'm just acknowledging my accountability. When I first figured it out, I was upset about it, but then I figured I had as much right to bite you as you did to bite me. It brought us mutual pleasure."

He couldn't deny the incredible pleasure, and

the need for more of the same. So Colin tried his best to be as accepting of the situation as Mia was trying to be—he knew she was still pretty rattled, even though she was trying to be objective. He rubbed his shoulder, aware of a sweet, phantom ache. The girl had sharp teeth for a mortal.

"And we did it a lot—tasted each other—even if I don't remember the times you bit me. I wonder why I don't remember?"

"We're stuck with each other," Mia said. "Till death do us part, I guess."

The vision of empty, lost, bondless David Berus flashed through Colin's mind. He shuddered at the thought of ending up like that. "Till death do us part," he told his bondmate. "And that will be a long long time."

"But you're immortal, and I'm—"

"Been watching *Buffy* reruns?"

"Right. Not immortal, just long-lived. Domini tried to explain that." He hadn't noticed that she'd put her head on his shoulder until she lifted it. "Domini also said something about my mysterious psychic talent being stimulated around you." She laughed. "You stimulate every other part of me. Could it be that when you made me forget, I bounced it back at you?"

He rubbed his chin. "I—suppose."

He wasn't sure if anything was settled, but fury wasn't buzzing between them anymore. That would have to do for now.

He stood and drew Mia to her feet. "We have plenty of time to explore our psychic connection later. Right now, we'd better get to the Matri's meeting before they send a commando team in for us."

Chapter Eighteen

"Nice," Laurent murmured, standing arrogantly in the center of the luxurious room. He looked around with the air of one who owned the place. "Very nice."

If there was one good thing to be said about the Clans, it was that they lived well. Not ostentatiously, mind you. Oh, no, the cultured, civilized, extremely old-money self-proclaimed good guys of the supernatural world had class, style, élan.

Laurent wanted to get him some of that. Or at least enough cold, hard cash to fake it. Being nouveau riche was fine with him.

In the meantime, he noted the tasteful paintings and sculptures, the numerous leather couches and chairs grouped around low tables, the subdued glow of the lighting, the rich color and texture of the carpet.

He was not unaware of the danger of the situation. Truce or not, he, Justinian, and Belisarius were standing in the den of their mother-loving enemies, with every Clan Prime in the territory ranged in a circle around the walls of the windowless room. No one had invited them to have a seat, of course. He supposed being offered a drink was out of the question.

And what exactly did Clan folk drink, anyway? It was a certain bet that their women didn't allow them to keep blood pets around the house. No way one of those poor, whipped bastards could just reach out and grab himself a hot one without Mama saying, "You put that mortal girl down right now!"

Laurent couldn't help but smile at the image, earning him a furious look from Belisarius.

"Relax," he whispered to the beta Prime. "So they have us outnumbered. We have—no, wait, we *don't* have right on our side. You may continue being terrified."

"I don't take commands from you."

Laurent managed to successfully hide his amusement this time, wondering if Belisarius realized just how stupid his automatic response sounded.

Justinian turned a fierce look on him. *This is taking too long, exile.*

Patience, my lord. We must be patient.

And wait on a woman's whim as to whether she will talk to me, and when?

Justinian's frustration at having to deal with the Clan women was understandable. It didn't help that they'd been kept waiting far longer than Elder Barak had promised. Laurent hoped the pack lord didn't blow their best chance out of impatience and outraged pride. Laurent gave a wary, assessing look at the Clan Primes ranged around the room. Though they weren't aware of it, Laurent recognized many of them. Every Prime in the city, except for the little Reynard shit who'd started this, was giving them cold, hard looks. The the Manticores would never get out of here if there was a fight.

Maybe even worse than the uneven numbers was the fact that the Clan vampires were memorizing their faces and psychic signatures. Hiding in this territory was no longer going to be possible.

"This had better work," he murmured, and drew dirty looks from the vampires he'd talked into coming here.

Before Justinian or Belisarius could say anything, a group of people entered the room. The Clan boys all straightened, practically coming to attention at the sight of several of their regal, proud women. The smallest of the lovely females seemed to be in charge. She was not young, but age only added a lovely patina to her beauty. She walked hand in hand with a barrel-chested male with dark skin for a vampire, and grizzled gray hair.

"Serisa and Barak of Shagal, aka Clan Jackal," Laurent said to Justinian.

He'd given the Manticores a briefing on the local players, but now he matched faces to the names. The Tribes were always amused and contemptuous of the humble scavenger names the Clans went by. Laurent figured the Clans saw their monikers as some kind of self-deprecating joke these grand chevaliers played on mortals and the rest of the supernatural world.

Not that this was the time to be analyzing names; his job was to get what they wanted and get out of here alive. A lot was going to depend on keeping Justinian and Belisarius from doing anything fatally stupid. They had both tensed at the sight of the female.

Be polite, he advised Justinian. *Be diplomatic. Or let me do the talking.*

Laurent knew his last comment was a big mistake even before Justinian gave him a poisonous look, for it was an implied challenge to the senior vampire's dominance.

Laurent bowed his head and took a quick step back.

Serisa spoke before Justinian reacted further. "Don't sneer at me if you want to get anything accomplished. I don't like dealing with you, either, but at least I don't resent you simply for your gender."

Justinian drew himself up haughtily. The Primes along the walls tensed. Then Justinian smiled, and swept Serisa an elegant bow.

"Forgive my rudeness. It's a bad habit I'll try not to indulge in in your presence. Our cultures are different, Lady, but my intent is to abide by the rules of your house, though I am not certain of all of those rules. Cut me some slack, please?" He spread his hands before him in a conciliatory gesture.

His last words held a certain charm, at least enough to make Serisa smile. Laurent noted that the smile didn't reach the shrewd old Matri's eyes. The Primes relaxed, but not much.

"A little slack," she agreed. "So we can get this over with as quickly as possible."

Justinian inclined his head with graciousness that took Laurent by surprise. "When you hear what I have to say, you will be glad you allowed this parlay, Matri."

"And why is that?" she asked.

Before he could answer, two more people entered the room, and everyone's attention turned toward the couple.

Well, well, well, isn't that sweet, Laurent thought. *They're holding hands.* He was willing to bet that they wouldn't be after the Clan brat found out the awful truth about his girlfriend.

No, not girlfriend, he realized as they came closer and the psychic energy that swirled between the pair permeated his own shielded senses. *Oh, shit! They're bonded!*

Bonding wasn't something the Tribes allowed, but Laurent had been around enough Clan and Family types to recognize the signs. He put a hand gently on Justinian's sleeve and telepathically pointed out this new wrinkle in the proceedings, while the lovebirds went to stand with the Matri's group.

Everyone was staring at her. She'd gotten stared at a lot the last couple of days and she was very uncomfortable with the looks she was getting from the trio in the center of the room—which included the blond vampire.

"You do know that's the one who attacked me, right?" she whispered to Colin.

He squeezed her fingers. "Oh, yeah," was his grim answer.

He aimed a murderous glare at the Tribe vampires, but didn't say anything as he led her to stand near Serisa and Barak. Domini was there, and Anjelica, along with a couple more Clan women and several older males. Mia felt young and way out of her depth in this crowd, and would have been happy to slip to the back behind everyone and not be noticed.

But apparently she and Colin were the center of attention. She wondered if they were ever going to be able to get away to start leading their lives and working out their relationship.

Serisa clapped her hands. "We are gathered in truce with our enemies," the Matri intoned.

Did the vampire leader have a ceremonial statement memorized for every occasion?

All the vampires, including the Tribe ones, clapped once. The combined effect was like a somber clap of thunder. Mia exchanged a glance with Domini, who claimed to be nominally human. Domini had her arms crossed, and she gave the faintest of shrugs when Mia caught her eye. Mia was almost reassured, knowing she wasn't the only one out of this particular ceremonial loop.

"Speak, Justinian of Manticore," Serisa said.

The one called Justinian took a step forward. Like all the other Primes she'd seen, Mia found him handsome, with a commanding presence. But unlike the Clan males she'd encountered, there didn't seem to be any sense of humor leavening the haughtiness of his bearing. He looked the way a vampire ought to: arrogant, cruel, and really, really pale.

"The Clans and Tribes disagree on almost every point," he began.

Justinian's voice was deep and compelling, and made her think of a high-powered trial lawyer. For some reason that image made Mia very uncomfortable—as if maybe she was the one on trial.

"Over the centuries, this has led us to misunderstand each other. But when it comes to the hunters, when it comes to survival of our kind, we are forced to cooperate." He produced a slick, sincere-seeming smile. "I have come to tell you that you are unknowingly harboring a female from one of the mortal bloodlines that have murdered our people for centuries."

"Would that be me?" Domini spoke up, taking a step forward and shielding Mia in the process. "If it is, you can leave now, because that thing with the Purist was settled long ago."

Justinian turned a look on Domini that could have melted titanium.

"Silence, female!" he snapped. Then he looked her up and down and sneered. "Mortal female, at that."

"So much for the civilized veneer," Domini murmured.

"Bi—" Justinian managed to stop himself before uttering the rest of the word.

The tension in the room escalated, and Alec moved forward. Tony Crowe put a hand on Alec's shoulder to stop him. The blond vampire did the same with Justinian.

Justinian shoved away his hand, but the blond turned to Serisa. "There's a story that needs to be told," he said hurriedly. "One that goes back several mortal generations. Allow us to tell you the root of our grievance and claim. We came here in good faith." He gave Domini a mildly reproachful look. "Bait a Prime of any of our kind, and he responds."

Domini frowned. "Okay. I did that." She pointedly did not address Justinian. "My apologies, Matri."

The friction among the Primes eased down a notch.

"Tell your story," Serisa directed.

The blond waited for a nod of permission from Justinian before he said, "For several centuries, a mortal family named Garrison pursued

Tribe Manticore. These murderers made it their mission to hunt us to extinction."

His words made Mia uncomfortable, and she could almost see their point of view.

"But the Manticore accepted the terms of the Great Truce of 1903," he went on. "We tried to pursue the peaceful coexistence promised by the truce. The Manticore disappeared into the night, to take blood as we need, but to live without killing. And the Garrisons retired from hunting. They still had the blood of our dead on their hands, but we vowed not to seek revenge. We lived by the truce." He looked around and asked, "Has anyone ever heard of a Manticore killing a mortal?"

After a short silence, Barak said, "Not for over a hundred years."

"When the truce freed us from the necessity of always being on the run, the Manticore finally had the time to amass a great deal of wealth. We used this wealth to protect our young, to try to fit into the modern world. We might have become one of those tribes that blended into the neutral ways of the Families."

Mia interpreted this statement as some sort of playing on the Clan vampires' sympathies, and it seemed to be working, at least a little.

"Whatever might have happened," he went

on, "we will never know. Because our future was destroyed by a man named Henry Garrison."

Oops, Mia thought, as shock rattled her.

Colin had put his arm around her shoulders; now it tightened in reaction to her psychic outburst.

"What?" he asked.

The blond went on, "Garrison was from the generation of the hunter family born after the truce was signed. He had no personal vendetta to pursue vampires, no reason to hunt us. But he came after us anyway. Not because of what we are, but because of what we had. This Garrison stole everything from us and made himself a wealthy man."

"A very wealthy man," Justinian added. "And Tribe Manticore has dedicated nearly a century to hunting him. It is our right to take back what is ours, but Garrison hides himself very well. It has taken us decades to find even a member of his family. And what do we encounter, when we finally have the key to his whereabouts within our reach? We find that the Clans have offered protection to this vampire murderer's great-granddaughter." He pointed at Mia. "To her."

Everyone turned to look at Mia.

"And by the way," the blond said, "these days, Garrison likes to be known as the Patron."

Chapter Nineteen

Colin's arm was no longer around her shoulder. In fact, he had stepped away and was the one looking at her with the most intent scrutiny.

Though the gazes turned on her were neutral and questioning, the psychic temperature in the room was decidedly cooler. And the air of danger was palpable just under the surface.

Mia went cold, and tried not to shake—but Good God, she was a mortal among vampires! And the blond had done a fine job of working the room.

She turned her glare on the Manticore vampires. "These are the ones who have been trying to kill me," she reminded the Clan members.

"We have been trying to—"

The blond hesitated, and Mia was willing to bet he was trying to come up with words that were more diplomatic than *capture, torture, interrogate.*

He settled on, "We have questions for the hunter. It was natural for us to approach her with a certain amount of caution."

"He jumped out of the bushes and grabbed me," Mia said. "If Colin hadn't rescued me, I don't know what would have happened." She glanced at Domini, then over at Alec and Tony. "And remember the attack in the parking garage?"

"We came here to claim our right to deal with the Garrison woman," Justinian said.

"She is now a member of Clan Reynard," Anjelica spoke up. "You cannot have her."

Mia flashed her Matri-in-law a shocked look. "What? Would you just turn me over to them otherwise?"

"We came to claim her," the blond said. "But we had no knowledge that the mortal had managed to connive to bond herself to a Prime. Of course, now our negotiations over the Garrison woman have become more complicated."

This guy was good. He was making it sound like she'd wormed her way into Colin's clan on purpose.

"My name isn't Garrison," she pointed out. "Henry Garrison *is* my great-grandfather, but—"

What was she supposed to say? That she'd only met the old boy a few days ago, that she didn't like him—and that he'd sent her out hunting vampires?

"I know very little about the man," she finished.

"He's richer than God, and about as old," Colin said. He took her by the arm. "That's what you told me about him once. Don't you remember?"

"Yeah—vaguely."

"You didn't tell me he's the Patron." His voice was soft, deadly, and very, very scary. So was the cold look in his eyes.

Being scared always made Mia angry. She jerked her arm away from Colin's grasp. "I didn't know."

Colin looked calm, but she was all too aware of the seething fury beneath the surface. "If you will excuse us, Matris, I need to talk to my bond-mate in private."

"Yes. We need a few minutes to work this out." Though *this* was so complicated, Mia had no idea how to begin.

"I protest," Justinian said. "This hunter-spawned female has her psychic claws in your young Prime. That makes him vulnerable to any poisonous lies she plants in his mind. It is the Manticores' right to question her. Let me—"

"You have ten minutes." Serisa cut him off. She made a shooing gesture. "Go out on the terrace and talk."

"When were you planning on telling me?"

Colin sounded far too calm, when she'd been waiting for an explosion. He'd been standing with his back to her for a couple of minutes, looking out at the landscaped hillside stretching down from the house. The marble terrace was empty; every sign of last night's celebration was gone.

Mia squinted in the bright light that poured down on them. She was aware of a growing headache, and wished for a pair of sunglasses.

She also wanted to go home.

She wanted her house, her profession, her life. She wanted to call her mom. She *definitely* didn't want anything to do with her great-grandfather.

"He ran out on my family," she reminded Colin. "Remember that I told you how he abandoned them? I didn't know anything about—no, that's not quite true. I knew about the Garrisons being hunters, but not about how he—"

"When were you going to tell me that you are a vampire hunter?" He turned slowly to face her. When she didn't immediately deny the charge, he lifted one heavily arched brow. "Well," he said, and put his hands behind his back. "Isn't this interesting?"

Mia would have preferred him to shout.

"Domini said I should tell you right away, but there hasn't exactly been time."

Surprised hurt spread from him like a shock wave. "Domini knew about this, but you didn't tell *me?*"

"There wasn't time!" Mia repeated. "The subject came up just before the ceremony." She crossed her arms and took a defiant stance in front of him. "And I don't know why I have to defend myself just because my ancestors and yours didn't get along. We're not the Hatfields and the McCoys, you know."

"Who?"

Okay, maybe Colin didn't know anything about American history. Or maybe it was mortal history he was weak on.

Mia tried another tack. "I'm not the enemy. I don't want to hurt anyone in the Clans."

Her own sincerity surprised her. It hadn't been so long ago that she'd lumped all vampires into the evil-monsters-that-must-be-destroyed category. What had changed her mind? Was it because they'd given her a beautiful dress and made her and Colin marry each other? Because they threw a great party? Maybe it was because the Clan vampires had defended her from the Tribe ones?

"Your people don't seem to have any kind of evil agenda toward humans. I haven't witnessed anything but your helping people." She looked at him with admiration. "You're a SWAT officer."

"Didn't you accuse me of using that to cover up killing people?"

She winced. "I was angry when I said that. Scared and totally confused at finding out you were a vampire."

"How could you be confused when you already knew about vampires?"

"I didn't know *you* were one! All I knew was what little my grandmother told me, which she learned from her grandfather and only half believed herself. A lot of information can get lost or garbled in that amount of time."

He looked thoughtful for a moment. "I guess mortals have a different view of time. What's within living memory for one of us can be ancient history for you."

She nodded. "Exactly. I knew I had a legacy, and a feeling I should do something about it, but—"

"Is that why you're such a jock? So you could kick vampire butt?"

She was embarrassed, since her training didn't stand up well against the reality of his kind. "I like being physical. But yeah," she admitted, "I've worked my butt off preparing for a scenario I never really thought would happen. And I certainly never intended to become a bad-ass vampire hunter until that blond guy jumped me."

"Tony said you were looking for the hunters." Colin slapped a hand to his forehead. "I am such an idiot. He kept saying you were a wannabe hunter. Why didn't I pay attention? Because I can't think around you." As if in proof, he grabbed her by the shoulders and drew her into a hard, fierce kiss.

She opened her mouth beneath his and responded just as fiercely. Heat raced through her, mutating the high drama of their argument into passion—deep physical and emotional need. She ran her hands down his back and thighs, reveling in the feel of warm skin and wiry muscles.

The kiss ended as abruptly as it began, leaving her dizzy with desire and totally frustrated. "Hey!"

He gave a harsh, breathless laugh and shook his head. "I can't think. All I want to do is that. And more."

"Me, too." She was crazy about Colin.

Or maybe just plain crazy. Here they were in

the middle of yet another argument, faced with a threat from those Manticore jerks, yet lust still sizzled and threatened to burn away all brain cells used for logical thought.

"We'd better not," she agreed. "Besides, you're still pissed at me."

"Yeah," he agreed.

"I still don't completely know why."

"Because of the Patron." Colin put his hands on her shoulders. "Don't you realize who this man is?"

"The man who deserted my grandmother's family," she responded. "This does not endear him to me. And apparently he got rich by stealing, but since that claim comes from vampires who attacked me, I'm not necessarily willing to believe that." But she couldn't deny that Henry Garrison and the Patron were the same man; she had heard one of his staff address him as Patron.

"Running out on your family and stealing from the Manticores are things he did in the past," Colin answered. "They're nothing compared to what the Patron is up to right now. He's a very, very dangerous man. Dangerous and sick, and ruthless."

Mia was stung, even if she didn't have much respect for Henry Garrison. "Dangerous and sick and ruthless is exactly what I thought about *your* relatives a couple of days ago. How can you say such things when you don't even know the man?"

"Oh, I know him," he answered. "I've taken a vow to destroy him."

"You what?" Mia jerked away and stared at her bondmate in horror. "I can't let you kill one of my relatives!"

"He's willing to kill mine."

"Yeah, but you're vampires—and he doesn't know any better. He's a traditionalist!"

"He's insane," Colin went on before she could protest further. "He doesn't care about saving the world from vampires. He wants to live forever. He thinks vampires are immortal, the way all hunters used to, and that he can steal the secret of immortality from us. And he has the money and mindset to pursue research into immortality. He uses mercenaries, and funds rogue scientists, kidnaps vampires and mortals, and has his scientists run hideous experiments on them."

She didn't believe she was hearing this. "That's the plot of a B movie. No one could get away with doing stuff like that."

"With enough money, you can get away with anything. The Clans have been funding private scientific research for a long time. In fact, your great-grandfather hired away several of our scientists for his research. I've been at the abandoned military base where the Patron's scientists ran their nasty experiments. I helped blow the place up. I helped rescue his prisoners. I was *there*, Mia. I know exactly how dangerous your relative is. He has to be stopped."

"But—"

He grabbed her shoulders again. For a moment she thought he was going to shake her, but he drew her close and stared intently into her eyes. "You're going to help me."

It was not a plea, nor was it a threat, but it was a cold, hard statement that would brook no argument.

She didn't try to argue, but she did say, "You could say please."

"Please."

Mia took a deep breath, and closed her eyes for a moment. She missed her preconceptions about vampires. It was so much easier to believe the crumbs she'd gleaned from family history, and what little her great-grandfather had told her. Right now, she felt like she was trying to pick her way through a minefield of conflicting realities. Everyone she'd met, every situation, gave her a different view of what it meant to be a vampire. But she had to make some hard choices.

To complicate things much more, now she was linked physically, emotionally, and psychically to a vampire, and to his clan.

Or at least that was what they wanted her to believe.

"My head hurts," she said. "It really does."

"I know." Colin's fingers moved to her temples and began a gentle massage. "Me, too."

"I want to go home."

"Me, too."

"And I'm sick of hearing about this Patron."

"*You're* sick of it? Sweetheart, he's been dominating my life for months. When I wasn't thinking about you, I was working on finding him. The closest I'd come to a lead was the night I ran into you at the airport, and—" His hands were suddenly back on her shoulders. "The airport—the same one the Patron's plane used. The same one you used."

Mia's heart slammed hard in her chest, and her stomach flip-flopped. She felt exposed, as if she was about to be accused of a horrible crime. Worse, she felt inexplicably guilty even before being accused.

"You're working with him!" Colin declared. "He found out I was the one hunting him, and he sent you to trap me!"

"Oh, for crying out loud!" she responded without thinking. "Why is it always about *you*?"

He laughed harshly. "I suppose it was a coincidence that we met when you were a hostage?"

"Yeah." Of course it was. It had to be. "Don't try to make me paranoid that my great-grandfather set up the worst day of my life so that I'd start dating a vampire! Then *you* followed *me* to the hospital, remember? And I didn't contact you after you broke up with me, did I?"

Her questions made him thoughtful. He looked away, then back at her. "Meeting me was the worst day of your life?"

He sounded dead serious, but there was a faint spark of teasing in his eyes. Maybe it was her "always about you" comment that had cut through his rising paranoia.

"Meeting you was—interesting. Being taken hostage that day was frightening." She looked around her. "Though I guess it was good practice for being kidnapped by vampires."

"We were both kidnapped by vampires," he reminded her. "What were you doing at that airport?" he went on, relentlessly back on the hunt. "And just how did you find Tony? Why? You *are* working for the Patron," he decided.

"Working with him," Mia answered. "Or at least, I thought I was." Colin gaped at her in surprise, which didn't help her already frayed temper. "You look like you thought I was going to lie to you and say, oh, no, I haven't had anything to do with the Patron. Come to think of it, I haven't. The man I went to for help, after I was attacked *by vampires,* is the only living relative I have who has ever had contact with vampires. I went to him for help," she reiterated.

"You could have—"

"Come to you?" Mia shook her head. "How could I? I was trying to *protect* you—from vampires."

When Colin started to laugh, Mia couldn't help but join him. Well, at the time she hadn't known how absurd that was.

They were still laughing when Barak appeared on the terrace and said, "Time's up."

Chapter Twenty

"Tell them," Colin said to Mia when they were once more standing before the Matris and the elders.

The Manticores stood at their back, but Colin had put himself between them and his bondmate. He realized with dread that no one in the room was going to like Mia's explanations, but the Manticores were the only ones that posed any real danger to her. The problem was, she couldn't really understand that yet.

Mia turned a confused look on him. "Tell them what?"

"Everything you know about the Patron," he clarified. "Everything you've done with him, or for him."

"Oh. Okay."

He'd thought she was going to protest. When she didn't he put a hand on her shoulder. It was meant to be reassuring—at least he tried to mean it that way. His head was still whirling from everything that had happened between them, the information overload of the last few hours. He was confused and furious—at Mia, because of Mia, for Mia.

But he was there for Mia. Whether she wanted him or not.

Mia took a deep breath, and focused on Serisa. "Henry Garrison is my great-grandfather. Until they attacked me"—she jerked a thumb over her shoulder—"I never had any contact with him. After the first attack, I knew I needed help fighting vampires. I didn't know how to contact the local vampire hunters. In fact, it didn't even occur to me at that time that I should try going that route. So I contacted Garrison."

"How?" Justinian demanded.

"With difficulty," she answered, without bothering to look at the Manticore Prime.

"And after you contacted him?" Serisa asked. "What then?"

"Then he asked me to bring him a vampire. For experimentation."

She said it without any hesitation, without any show of fear. Colin wasn't the only one in the room who gasped.

"You're working for the Patron?" Domini

asked. "You're helping him with his sick research?"

"I didn't know it was sick at the time, did I?" Mia asked in turn. "He told me he wanted to learn more about vampires, that he wanted one to study. He didn't say anything to me about research into immortality."

"What about our money?" the blond Manticore asked. "Did he mention anything about where he keeps large sums of stolen cash?"

"There are more important things than money," Serisa declared.

The blond gave a derisive snort of laughter.

"What about our claim?" the leader of the Manticores spoke up. "The Garrison woman can lead us to what is ours, what was stolen by a mortal. Is it not our right to question her, under the agreements established to protect our kind from vampire hunters?"

"The Patron posses a threat to all our kind," Barak said. "You have the right to assist in the hunt for him."

"What if the female won't help you?" Justinian persisted. "If you deem finding Garrison important for all vampires, but the woman won't cooperate, what then? We have a claim on her information; you must allow us what is ours by right."

Colin spun around to bare his fangs at the

Manticore Primes. "Do you know how much I will enjoy killing all of you, if you try to touch what is *mine*?"

"Well, excuse *me* for having a free will and the ability to make my own decisions."

Colin whirled back around to find Mia standing with her arms crossed and a look of complete disgust on her face.

She turned slowly, aiming her annoyance at everyone in the room, and didn't speak until she was looking at him again. "Perhaps it would be nice if someone would kindly *ask* me to help," she suggested.

"Good point," Domini spoke up.

Silence loomed with a tense crackle, like the still air before the explosion of a thunderstorm.

Finally, Anjelica asked, "Will you help us, Caramia?"

Mia sighed, and her shoulders slumped, but she put her hand out to stop him when Colin move to come toward her. The weariness and worry that emanated from her disturbed him, no matter how infuriating she was. She faced the women of the Clans.

"Let me think about it," she answered them. "Just give me some space to think."

"No!" Justinian protested.

Serisa studied Mia for a few moments, her

expression was both worried and calculating. Finally she said, "Very well."

"Wait, wait, wait, just like the Matri wants."

Colin glanced at the newcomer and reluctantly answered. "If you don't like it, leave."

"My master has chosen to remain. I live to serve, and all that. How about you? Do you always do what you're told?"

Colin had been sitting alone on a bench at the back of the garden when the blond Manticore Prime came strolling down the path. He'd been out here for a couple of hours, long enough to watch the sky go through a fine pastel sunset and to watch stars and moon come out. He hadn't exactly been enjoying the solitude, but this was one of the last people he wanted interrupting his thoughts.

"Do you always hang out where you're not wanted?" Colin answered. He'd been told the pest was named Laurent. "It's after sunset. Why don't you people leave?"

"Justinian won't go until he has what he wants." Laurent took an uninvited seat on the bench. "Think of me as his interpreter of the modern world. You wouldn't like Justinian without me around."

"I don't like Justinian anyway."

"Ah, but he's on his best behavior at the

moment. He's much worse than you imagine—which makes us quite proud of him. But since you boys don't seem to have a handle on decadence, perversion, and guile, you need my help pointing it out to you. He needs me to keep reminding him how upright, upstanding, and honest you folks really are. Frankly, I don't know how you good guys manage to have any fun."

"Nobility has its boring side," Colin conceded. "But the dragon slaying"—he bared his teeth in a smile—"a manticore's a type of dragon, isn't it? and rescuing the fair maiden has its rewards."

Laurent stretched his long legs out in front of him. "If I read the signs aright, there's no more maiden-rescuing in your future. Not that your woman isn't lively enough in bed, I suppose, but to be stuck with only one . . ."

"I could happily kill you, you know."

"It'd give you something to do. This place is nice, but dull."

"You've got that right."

Maybe he was tired and wired, or maybe he missed the mocking camaraderie of his SWAT unit, but Colin almost found the Tribe vampire's attitude amusing. He didn't forget the guy was everything mortal legends thought vampires were, though, or that he was at the Citadel because of an agenda that could threaten Mia.

"But while our attempting to kill each other would be diverting, that would be breaking the truce, as I am speaking in friendship," Laurent went on.

"And how is that?"

"I was only offering my condolences on your bonded state, one Prime to another—as we of the Tribes don't believe that monogamy is the natural condition for a Prime. Do you know how we avoid the bonding state?"

"No."

"Do you care?"

"Does it involve violence toward women?" Colin asked, quietly and dangerously serious. His fists were clenched to fight the urge to strike.

Laurent studied him carefully for a moment. "Maybe I shouldn't have brought up the subject."

"I guess not." He forced himself to relax a little.

"She's a dangerous woman, you know."

Colin smiled. "I know."

Laurent shook his head. "Can you control her?"

"That's none of your business."

"Do you think you can trust her?" These words were spoken with far more seriousness than anything else the Manticore had said. "She's Garrison's," Laurent went on. "Your blood is in her, but so is the Patron's DNA." He stood and moved away. "Can a bond overcome birth? Where does her loyalty really lie?"

With those words, Laurent faded into the night. Tribe members were the masters of vanishing into shadows. For all their bad habits, they had a certain dark style.

And he left Colin with dark thoughts. He tried to let Laurent's words roll off him, to remember that the Manticore was working his own agenda. Of course, that didn't make everything Laurent said a lie. And there was the matter of trust.

One thing that bothered Colin was how worried Mia had been about having her deeper thoughts read. Fear of violation? Or was she hiding some plan of the Patron's? He didn't know, and he hated thinking about it.

It had been a rough couple of days, and it just got rougher and rougher.

Colin tiredly stretched out on the bench and stared up at the night sky for a while. He drifted off for a while, but restless need wouldn't let him sleep.

After a while he stood up, stretched, and headed back toward the house. "That's it. Time's up. She's had enough time to think."

A sense of panic drove Mia to sit up and look around frantically. She heard someone move. "Colin?"

"No," Domini answered from what seemed a long way away.

Mia blinked and rubbed her eyes. It had been dark, and she'd been dreaming and— "Was I asleep?"

"Yes."

Domini sounded very calm, reassuring. Mia looked toward her. Domini was on the couch on the other side of the bedroom where Mia had been kept before the bonding ceremony. It took Mia a few more moments to piece together the memory of being shown in here and left alone.

She rubbed her eyes again. "I was supposed to be thinking, but I think I just crawled into bed and passed out."

"You needed the rest," Domini answered. "They don't need to sleep as much as we do, so they'll run us ragged without realizing it."

"How long was I out?"

"Maybe three hours. Not long, but maybe long enough to help you think straight." Domini gestured toward a covered tray on a low table near her. "There's tea and food. Would you prefer coffee?"

Mia got out of bed and crossed the room. Taking a seat in one of the chairs, she eyed Domini. "Did they send you to talk to me because you're a mortal who's bonded to a vampire? Are you going to convince me that I can trust you because we have so much in common?"

Domini reached over and flipped the tray covering. The scent of Earl Grey tea perfumed the air, and Mia's stomach began to rumble at the sight of a plate of sandwiches, and another one piled with fancy cookies.

"We do have a lot in common," Domini said, not seeming concerned at Mia's suspicious attitude. "Though I'm not *exactly* mortal." She looked Mia in the eye and added with quiet intensity, "And it is all about trust."

Mia poured herself a cup of tea, spooned in sugar, then snatched up half a sandwich. It was ham and cheese, and she ate it in three bites. Then she gulped down the wonderfully warm, sweet tea. She tried the cookies next.

She sighed when she was done, and the plates were mostly empty. "What do you mean, not exactly?" she asked, looking the other woman over curiously. "Are you turning into a vampire?" A jolt of alarm ripped through her. "Will I?"

Domini gave her a stern look. "Even the most amateur hunters know better than that."

Mia let out a relieved sigh. "Okay, I forgot that one for a moment. But if you're not—"

"I will eventually become a vampire," Domini said. "It's rare, but it sometimes happens. But the only reason I can change is because my grandmother is a vampire. My grandfather is mortal. And—here's where what you and I have in common comes in—he's from a family of hunters. Actually, he's from a family of Purists." When Mia looked at her blankly, she said, "You don't know about the Purists?"

"I know very little about hunters," Mia said.

"You were trying to find them, Tony said. But you didn't know where to find them?"

Mia nodded.

"That tells me that your great-grandfather has no interest in legally hunting rogue vampires. Tony is our local liaison with the hunters. Since we found out the Patron's name, Tony has been trying to find out if the hunters know anything about Garrison. Though they have the family name in their database, no one has heard of him. If he's so rich and wants to hunt vampires, why send an untrained female out alone, when there are official resources he could contribute to?" She clasped her hands over a raised knee, and tilted her head to one side. "My guess is that the old man set you up as bait. But you need to make up your own mind about him."

Mia poured herself more tea and gave Domini a skeptical look. "Then what are you here to influence me about?"

Domini smiled. "About your place in vampire society."

"You mean about where my loyalties should lie?"

"About trust. You have to make up your mind who deserves your trust."

Mia put the fine china cup down so hard it rattled the other dishes. "Hey! I don't know you."

"You know me better than you do your great-grandfather. At least you've spent more time with me."

Mia had to nod her agreement to this.

"I know that Earl Grey is your favorite tea—and that when Colin offers you the choice, you're going to take the ruby instead of the diamond."

"What?"

"Sorry." Domini tapped her forehead. "Having a psychic episode. I get flashes of future events. Junk stuff, usually. But that brings me back to how hunters and vampires are really a lot alike, and how this knowledge will help you make a more informed decision about helping find the Patron."

"How are hunters and vampires alike?"

"There's a lot of psychic talent in both groups, and they intermarry a lot more than either will admit." She held up a hand and leaned forward earnestly while Mia digested this information. "But the decision about the Patron is still yours."

Mia remembered how adamant Colin had been about her helping him on his Patron-smashing quest. "You think so?"

"Oh, the boys will huff and puff and try to guilt you into living up to their noble ideals, and Colin will be the worst. But they won't *make* you do what they want. They are the good guys."

"The Manticores aren't good guys."

"No," Domini agreed. "The Manticores, and the other Tribes like them, are one of the reasons that some mortal vampire hunters still exist. The Tribes are the reason that the Purists still hunt all vampires, and that even the more reasonable hunters will never completely trust the Clans or the Families. As long as the Purists exist, vampires can never completely trust mortals. People like Garrison, people who use anybody for their own selfish reasons, just make it harder for everybody to trust anybody." Domini uncurled herself from the couch and stood. "But the point is still, who do you trust? Who's your family? And what are you going to do about it? That'll be Colin," she added, just before a knock sounded on the door.

Mia watched Domini open the door and glide out as Colin entered and announced, "We have to talk."

Chapter Twenty-one

"*O*h, for crying out loud! Hasn't there been enough talking? There's a couple of ham sandwiches left," Mia added as her bondmate crossed the room.

He was wearing jeans and a tight black T-shirt that emphasized his leanly muscled body, and she couldn't help but appreciate how good he looked. They'd only been separated for a few hours, but seeing him sent a surge of longing through her. More than a strong physical reaction, a sense of security blossomed up from some deep part of her now that he was with her.

The front part of her brain could argue that this was a false sense of well-being, but it didn't argue hard at the moment. Besides, it had never been the front part of her brain that was attracted to Colin. She'd gone on instinct with him from the first.

Which was probably not good in the long

run. Or was instinct what mattered? Where did trust come from? The gut, or the logic center of the brain?

It's lust, she reminded herself. It rhymes with trust, but it's not the same thing.

And just where does the heart come into it?

"How's the thinking coming along?" he asked.

"I think I'm thinking too much about anatomy," she answered. "Or maybe it's philosophy. Either way, it doesn't make any sense."

"Anatomy, huh?" He picked up a sandwich and settled on the wide arm of her chair. "What did Domini want?" he asked around a bite of food, and put a hand on her shoulder. The contact between them was as electric as ever, even if he had been touching her like this an awful lot lately. There was something proprietary about this touch, this one spot of contact that linked him to her.

She leaned sideways, letting her shoulder and head touch his side. His hand moved from her shoulder to the back of her neck, and his thumb began to work at muscles she hadn't realized were tense.

"Domini was being a cheerleader for your side," she answered.

"My *side*?"

She sighed, partly in exasperation, partly

because what he was doing felt good. "Oh, don't get all huffy."

"Have you picked a side yet?"

"I've been adopted into Clan Reynard, haven't I?"

"Bonded."

"It's the same thing."

It amazed her that neither of them were speaking these words in anger. There was tension between them, all right, but her body was growing tight with desire.

"Have you thought about the Patron?"

"Some. Mostly I took a nap."

"That wasn't very productive."

"I dreamed about you."

"As you should. Was I naked?"

She gave a snort of laughter, and as she did, Colin somehow managed to slide down from his perch to squeeze himself beside her in the plush armchair. It was a tight fit, one that made her pleasantly aware of every bit of Colin's hard, toned body.

"We need to talk," he said, and kissed the back of her neck. Then his lips brushed the side of her throat, and up to her ear.

The breath caught in her throat, but Mia managed to say, "Keep doing that, and we won't be able to talk."

Wanna bet?

She laughed. Not out loud, but inside her head, sharing her amusement with him on the psychic level. Desire bubbled up from the laughter, and burst like sparks that heated from the soul out to the skin.

It's been hours, he thought. *I missed you.*

She felt the truth in the thought.

Who would have thought the truth could be so sexy? It sent desire rippling through her in a way that was strong, deep, and devastating. There was a new level calling to her here. A challenge to go beyond everything she'd experienced before.

Mia liked challenges.

I like you thoughtful, Colin.

Colin. The name had taste and texture, color and depth, in her mind. Sweet, spicy taste, scarlet silk and sharp iron entwined in texture, shifting changing color of fire.

Caramia.

He thought her name, and she became aware of his response to her—the velvet touch of yellow roses, the taste of cinnamon candy, warm coffee with cream and lots of sugar, the rush of wind during free fall.

All the great guitar solos ever played burned through them: Eric and Carlos and Jimi and Lenny and—

After a while, Mia managed to pull back into herself enough to think, *This is so, so—*

Psychedelic?

Yeah. Don't you have any Coldplay in there? Me, I like Metallica.

She found her voice. "Does this sort of thing happen often?"

"I don't know—I'm new here." His voice sounded raw with desire, with emotions he'd never known before.

Mia knew how he felt. Not only because she felt new herself, but because they were bound together. They were in this together.

She opened her eyes, to find herself gazing into Colin's. And she realized that her eyes hadn't been closed; they'd just been lost in each other.

"Nice," she said.

He pulled her into his lap, and his hand came up under her shirt to stroke her breasts. "Nicer," he said.

His fingertips barely touched her, barely moved, spreading a slow fire from the outside in.

He held her still, not letting her move. And he kept on caressing and kissing her with the slowest and gentlest of touches. He stripped her of her clothes, but without any hurry, thoroughly stimulating every new bare spot, taking delight in learning her responses. He took such delight in her body, it was as if he was discovering her sensuality for the first time.

It made her feel like this was their first time, as well.

But Colin's subtlety kept her a millisecond away from the desperately desired cataclysm, driving her crazy.

Before long, she was begging him for more.

"More?"

He loved being in control of her pleasure— and it was fine with her.

"*More.*" She let out a long, desperate moan. *Everything. Anything.* "*Colin!*"

His triumphant laugh bubbled through her like champagne. He picked her up and swung her around with a speed more than human, so fast that the room swirled into blurred colors. She threw her head back against his shoulder and let the roller-coaster ride take her even further away from herself, further into her need for him.

She was dizzy in every possible way when he finally dropped her on the bed.

"This is like skydiving without a chute!" She held her arms up toward him.

He undressed so quickly, she was only aware of a blur and of clothes being tossed all over the room.

Colin was laughing when he dropped on top of her. His mouth covered hers even as she gasped. His tongue swirled and teased, drawing her even further toward rapture. But the kiss didn't last nearly long enough.

Using more of his natural strength and speed, he flipped them over, switching their positions. Now he was on his back, and she was poised over him. His hands held her waist, and her legs were on either side of him, her knees pressed against his narrow hips.

Mia could feel the tip of his cock straining upward, barely grazing the wet and swollen entrance of her sex, sending jolts of heat deep inside her. She instinctively tried to move her hips downward, to join his body with hers. All she wanted in the world was him in her, to be filled. It was a hunger like nothing she'd ever known before.

But he wouldn't let her move.

She arched her back, felt his cock twitch in response.

"Colin!" she complained. "You're going crazy, too!"

He gave a dark and sexy laugh. "Yep."

"Why are you doing this?"

Because I can.

He was loving the control, and holding on to

it with all his might. And he was loving her responses to that control. She'd never been more aware of her body, of the cravings that only Colin could excite and satisfy. Her breasts were heavy, her nipples aching. Her nerve endings were on fire, and coiling heat burned inside her. There was no blood craving involved right now, but the lust was all-consuming.

"Colin!" she pleaded. "Enough!"

He was covered in a sheen of sweat, muscles tautly straining, his dark eyes glittering, and he was shaking from holding back. "You want me?"

"Yes!"

His smile was dangerous. His voice was low, and commanding. "Make it slow."

His hands came away from her hips, and moved to cup her breasts. The shock wave that went through her when his thumbs grazed her nipples would have set off an orgasm, but Colin's voice in her head murmured, *Easy.*

Mia lowered her body onto his cock, taking him into her with the slowness he commanded. A climax wracked through her with every little movement, but somehow she found the willpower to take him the way he wanted, though she was screaming inside for pounding speed.

She kept on stroking him, setting a slow, slow,

sliding rhythm for a long, long time. She brushed her breasts across his chest, joined her mouth to his on every downstroke. She twined her tongue with his with hot, fleeting kisses. Their breathing grew more and more ragged, the connection between them more electric.

His hands roamed over her, stroked her clitoris, bringing her to another climax. When she moaned, the groan that came from deep in his throat matched her sound.

She couldn't stop her response to that heartfelt groan, and her hips ground down hard against his. He bucked as she plunged.

His orgasm took her with the same explosive intensity as it did him.

The next thing Mia knew, she was lying stretched out on top of Colin, and he was holding her as she shook like a leaf.

"It's okay," he murmured, lips close to her ear. "It's—that was—"

"*Wow,*" she finished for him. For some reason there were tears stinging her eyes. Tears of joy, of exhaustion, of release, tears for all sorts of reasons. She couldn't ever remember crying over great sex before. She wiped her face against Colin's shoulder, surprised that she wasn't uncomfortable showing this vulnerability. But if the man could get inside her head, and she into his—

Mia fell asleep before this thought was complete.

She was called out of very pleasant warm darkness when Colin shifted and said, "We're going to be in trouble for keeping the Matris waiting."

For a moment, still foggy with sated lust and bone-melted exhaustion, Mia didn't have a clue what he was talking about. She didn't even remember where they were, other than a very comfortable bed.

Then the whole mess came back to her, and she sighed and sat up. Colin was propped up on a pile of pillows, one arm thrown over his head, and he didn't look at all guilty for keeping the tribunal waiting. She couldn't help but trace a finger around the unrepentant smile quirking his lips.

"Didn't you say you wanted to talk to me when you came rushing in here?"

His eyes narrowed in thought. "Oh, yeah . . . the Patron. How are you going to help me save the world from him?"

She noted that he wasn't asking if she'd help. "Can I ask you a question?"

"And waste more time before we have to face the honorable old ladies?" He propped his other hand behind his head, and grinned. "Sure."

Anjelica and Serisa sure didn't look like old

ladies to her, but Mia let that go. "Why do you want to save the world?" she asked seriously. "You really believe in the hero mystique, don't you? Why do vampires protect humans?"

"Mortals," he corrected. He looked at her breasts and smiled happily for a moment before pulling his gaze back up to her face. "Vampires are humans, too—superior humans, sexier and more virile humans. Mortals need protection from themselves, and from—"

"Morally superior, horny vampire snobs."

"No, no." He shook his head. "We snobs take vows to protect and serve."

"But why? How long has this been going on? What do you get out of it?"

He gave her a hard look. "Will the answers help you make up your mind about the Patron?"

She supposed she couldn't put it off much longer. She swallowed, and steeled her resolve. "Yes."

"For one thing, taking care of mortals is fun. It beats Primes fighting each other for dominance and territory. The matris and elders figured out a long, long time ago that we need outlets for aggression. I learned in vampire school—"

"You have vampire school?"

"You don't think I went to Harvard, do you?"

"I don't think you could get into Harvard."

"I went to UCLA." He caressed her cheek. "I learned in vampire school that the Clans' protection of mortals started being codified back in ancient Egypt—something about a bunch of vampires being saved from some disaster by priests of Osiris, and taking a vow before the god of death to protect the priests and their families."

"Nice legend."

"I don't think it's a legend—there's written records of this pact someplace. It's the basis for the code we live by. Some of us." He held out his left arm to show her the fox head tattooed on the inside of his wrist. She'd noticed it before. "Those of us who serve mortals take the vow and wear the mark of our Clan."

"So nobody makes you do it."

He nodded. "And there have always been perks to the job."

"Damsels in distress taste delicious."

"They certainly do. And I guess there were Primes who protected ancient cities and were treated as gods for it. It's a pretty good life—you kick the occasional bad guy's ass, and get to live in a palace and have all the women you want in return."

"Too bad that times changed."

"And as times changed, the Families got into leading mostly normal lives, but the Clan Primes went into a tragically misunderstood gothic hero period." He looked pained. "I am so glad I wasn't around for that. I suspect they wore poet shirts and black capes when they appeared out of the night to save the damsels."

Mia grinned. "Not your style."

"And then politics came into the picture, complicating the choices between good and bad. My own family worked on both sides of the French Revolution. Some saved the aristocrats from the evil peasants; some saved the downtrodden peasants from the decadent aristocrats. There was a lot of damsel tasting on both sides."

Mia laughed. "Vampire family feuds can't be pretty."

He shook a finger at her. "We're Clan."

"You know what I meant."

"Yes. But the distinction between Clan, Family, and Tribe is important."

"Why?"

He looked surprised, and opened his mouth a couple of times before he answered. "The Tribes are bad guys. Always have been, always will be."

"Didn't the blond guy say something about Tribes having blended into the Families?"

"Yeah, but I wasn't listening too hard."

She remembered that he'd been busy trying not to show how pissed at her he was on finding out she was involved with hunters and the Patron. She didn't want him pissed at her now. She would much rather have conversations than arguments with Colin.

"What about Clan Primes in the modern era?" she asked.

Colin was aware of Mia's mental barriers going up, though he hoped she wasn't consciously aware of doing it. He suspected part of her sudden distancing herself was because of the damsel in distress comments. They likely reminded her of his reluctance to be permanently involved with a mortal woman. It was a fact, and there was no use arguing about it any more.

"You know about modern Primes," he told her.

She moved across the wide bed and stood up, putting mental distance from him as she moved away. "We better talk to your people now."

She sounded reluctant and unhappy. Her nervousness sang against his senses. She didn't trust that the Primes were right about the Patron, did she? Her lack of trust reminded him of what Laurent had said about trusting the kin of the Patron.

Right now, all he wanted was to fulfill his vow to destroy the threat the old man posed, then get on with his life. A Prime fulfilled his vows, no matter the consequences and complications to his own life.

But how could he make a mortal woman understand that no matter how much they talked about the history of the Primes?

"Yeah," he answered Mia, getting out of the opposite side of the bed. "It's about time we had that talk."

Chapter Twenty-two

"This is taking too long," Justinian complained.

He got up and began to pace around the dining room where the Manticores had been invited by their Clan hosts, after hours of being kept in the meeting room. Laurent's senses told him it was past dawn, though the room was windowless.

Another day living in the lap of luxury—if the Clan mamas don't decide to kill us or toss us out to fry.

"We are being treated as guests," he carefully advised the impatient pack leader. "We must have patience."

"Patience is for the weak Clans. Do they always talk and never act?"

Laurent shrugged.

Belisarius glared across the table at Laurent,

then got up and went to stand against a wall. From there he kept his attention on Justinian, playing the loyal subordinate vigilant on his master's behalf.

Laurent stayed in his seat and continued to sip his dinner. The warmed wine mixture was beyond excellent. In fact, it was the best blood he'd ever had outside its natural container. There were subtle flavors in the mixture that he couldn't identify. Possibly the brew was laced with some of the drugs the Clans favored.

Drugs that helped them dwell in the daylight? He doubted they'd offer what they considered a gift to Tribe vampires. Especially knowing that the Manticores would pitch a fit, feeling that their bodies were polluted. Well, Justinian would, and Belisarius would follow his lead. More likely, the drugs Laurent tasted were those that helped the Clans keep their blood cravings to a minimum.

Laurent could understand why they might want to feed those drugs to dangerous, uncivilized Tribe members. In his opinion it was akin to chemical castration, but one dose wasn't going to permanently fix him, so there was no use getting mad about it. Not when it tasted so good. He looked at the goblet after he finished the last sip and placed it on the table.

Could he get a second glassful? Would it be bad for him?

He wondered how long the Clan members could go between natural feedings using the stuff, and why they wanted to. He could understand the advantages of dwelling in daylight, even if other Tribe members couldn't, but voluntarily turning yourself into a eunuch? He shuddered. Did they do it for the sake of living more openly among mortals? Because they really believed that creatures of the darkness could be *good*? Hell, it wasn't as if a vampire had to kill mortals to take their blood—though draining the life out of helpless victims was an appealing prospect.

Laurent smiled.

"Too long!" Justinian shouted.

Laurent looked up to see that the door had opened, and Justinian had yelled at Matri Serisa as she walked in.

"I agree," she said serenely, and took a seat at the head of the table.

Several people followed her into the room, among them the Garrison woman and her Prime keeper. Laurent hoped the fact that the pair weren't touching or looking at each other was good for the Manticore cause. The group took seats around the table, leaving the chair to

Serisa's right for Justinian. The Garrison woman sat on the Matri's left.

Justinian glared at everyone for a few moments, then stalked over and took his seat. "Well?" he demanded.

Serisa looked to her left.

"I'm willing to help." The mortal woman looked at Serisa when she spoke.

"Willing?" Justinian growled. He brought the flat of his hand down on the shining wood of the table. "The female should not be allowed to speak, let alone set conditions."

Mia looked at Justinian, temper flaring in her eyes. "You're a rude jerk, but I'll help you get your money back."

Justinian smiled, showing fangs. "And will you *help* with our revenge as well?"

"Oh, cut out the melodrama," Foxe said.

Laurent schooled his features and emotions, not wanting to show that he completely agreed with the Clan Prime.

"Of course I'm not helping you get revenge," Mia said. She looked around at everyone at the table. "If my great-grandfather is doing bad things, I'll help you stop him."

"Bad things?" Colin Foxe echoed. "Hon—"

Serisa gestured him to silence. "How will you

help us and Tribe Manticore?" she asked Mia. "Will you tell us where to find him?"

"I'll take you to him," Mia answered. She looked at Foxe. "I'll get you in to talk to him, search his compound, whatever you need to stop his operation. But you can't kill him," she added. "I won't let you kill my great-grandfather."

"That is unacceptable," Justinian said.

Laurent thought that Justinian spoke just before Foxe would have said the same thing.

"He's an old man," Mia said. "He's in his nineties. Maybe that's not old to your kind, but among ours that makes him ancient. He isn't going to live that much longer."

"Which is why he's trying to find the secret to immortality," Foxe pointed out.

"But there isn't one. So, you shut down his experiments, destroy the research records. You make him forget vampires exist. Do whatever you have to do, short of killing him. You have to promise that," she insisted, concentrating her plea on Colin Foxe.

While Justinian seethed and Belisarius fought the urge to attack the Garrison woman from behind, Laurent decided it was time to get back to the important point. "We don't care about the Patron's medical experiments. We want our money back."

Mia flashed him a smile. "And that's the solution right there. Take away my great-grandfather's wealth, and he can't fund any mad scientist stuff."

"And how can you give us his wealth?" Justinian demanded. "Do you know where he keeps a vault full of gold?"

"No, but I know where he keeps his laptop," the woman answered tartly. "If you can't find out how to break into his financial records with that, you really are a bunch of pathetic medieval losers, aren't you?"

After a moment of shocked silence, Justinian mastered his outrage and sneered at her. "And we are supposed to trust *you* to bring us this laptop?"

"Yes."

Justinian laughed. "Such calculating openness, such false naïveté. We do not forget the female's treacherous blood." He looked earnestly at Serisa. "Do you? Do you really think she will betray her blood?"

"She will bring the laptop to us," Serisa answered, ignoring Justinian's skepticism. "We will share whatever information we find about the Patron's finances with you."

Justinian banged his hand on the table again.

"This is where you're going to have to compromise, Matri," Laurent said before Justinian broke into a rage that could turn violently ugly. "From our point of view, you have just told us that you will take charge of the wealth that was stolen from us. You say *share information,* but what we hear is *take what is ours.*"

"Don't the Clans have enough wealth already?" Justinian demanded. "Are you so contemptuous of the Tribes that you would stoop to stealing from us?"

Serisa's head snapped up proudly. "Of course not!"

Justinian gave a satisfied nod. "Then you cannot object to my sending one of my Primes to retrieve this laptop for us."

Finally, Serisa nodded.

Justinian looked at Laurent. "You."

Belisarius stepped forward. "But he—"

"Laurent goes," Justinian snapped. "Understood?"

Awestruck by the possibilities, Laurent was unaffected by the glares being turned on him not just by Belisarius, but by Fox and the woman, as well. He was also fully aware that Justinian's question had been aimed him, and of its dangerous implications.

"Understood," he answered. He smiled at

Foxe. "So, partner, when do we assault the Patron's fortress?"

"No assault!" Mia waved her hands. "No violence. Nobody gets hurt."

"He's surrounded by security, isn't he?" Foxe asked.

"All rich people have bodyguards. They're just doing their jobs to protect him."

"We do not want innocent casualties," Serisa said.

"The Patron uses well-armed, trained mercenaries," Foxe said. "I've fought them; I know what they can do."

"That was a different time and place." Barak spoke for the first time. "You destroyed his private army. We do not know if he has had time to rebuild his organization. Mia could be correct about the people currently guarding the Patron. We will approach this operation with an initial nonlethal action plan."

"Aw," Laurent complained, and got an agreeing look from Foxe.

"*Initially* nonlethal?" Mia protested.

"We cannot go in unprepared," Barak told her.

"You can't do anything without me," she pointed out, and crossed her arms. "And I have a plan."

Chapter Twenty-three

Everybody's going to be really pissed at me if this doesn't work, Mia thought as the car approached the rendezvous point at the Van Trier airport.

She and Colin were seated on opposite sides of the spacious back seat, not touching. They hadn't spoken for a while, either, not even by telepathic contact. Ever since the op started, Colin had been focused on nothing else.

To set everything in motion she'd made a phone call, and they'd been picked up by a car sent by her great-grandfather's lawyer. So far, so good, but those who'd argued against doing it her way weren't going to like it if anything went wrong.

Colin had been one of the one's who argued about her coming along, no matter how necessary her presence was. She didn't know whether he was trying to protect her, or if it was because once the action got started, Primes were macho males who ran the show. She had a nagging fear that he didn't quite trust the Patron's great-granddaughter. And she almost didn't blame him if that were the case.

Even more important, if her plan didn't work, people and vampires both could end up dead. She wanted no deaths on her conscience.

Well, maybe the smart-mouthed blond Manti-core guy.

No, not even him.

"What a rough, tough slayer I made," she whispered, and got a quelling look from Colin in response.

She quelled the impulse to stick out her tongue, since Colin's gaze flicked briefly toward the driver. The driver ultimately worked for the Patron. The less gratuitous chatter, the better, if this make-shift undercover operation was to work.

Colin was half tempted to reach over, pat Mia's hand, and reassure her that she would do just fine. She might not be up to slaying vampires, but she could hold her own in a fight against mortal opponents.

He was spoiling for a fight, but he had to hope that it didn't come to one. One of the reasons he hadn't wanted Mia along was that if she got into trouble, his first impulse would be to protect his bondmate. That impulse could cloud his judgment in the middle of a dangerous situation. And maybe another reason he didn't want her in a fight was because he wasn't sure which way her instincts would impel her to jump.

But he admitted that her presence was necessary. She was the key. But having her with him was dangerous in many ways. Not only did he worry about her safety, he had trouble keeping his hands off her. This was not a situation where a Prime's natural lust for his bondmate was welcome. Not touching her was a misery, but it was the only choice for now.

"Remember to stay in character," he'd told her before they left the house. "Keep your hands to yourself and your mind on business."

His tone and attitude had angered her. "Do I look like a lust-crazed idiot to you?"

"Yes," he'd answered, not adding that he was even more crazed than she was. It was better to have her pissed at him and in character, even if having her angry brought its own dangers.

Now, as the car pulled to a stop next to another dark sedan, he chafed at not being in charge of the situation, but tried to tell himself that this was no different than an op led by his mortal SWAT commander. Except that he had total faith in his commander's abilities.

"Let's go," he said.

Mia steeled her resolve at Colin's words, trying to emulate his calm. She got out of the car and approached the man standing at the rear of the other car, recognizing him as one of the lawyers she'd dealt with before.

"Where is the object?" he asked when she reached him. Then he looked suspiciously at Colin. "Who is this?"

Mia was pleased with the man's reaction; he obviously didn't recognize Colin for a vampire. She'd been worried that there was some secret way his nature could be detected, and now she was a bit more confident this would work.

"He's here to help," she told the lawyer. She gestured toward the trunk of the car she and Colin had come in. "We brought what my great-grandfather requested."

"You'll want to verify the merchandise," Colin said. He made it sound like a drug deal.

He walked to the back of the car, and she and the lawyer followed. The lawyer looked nervous.

Mia was now glad that she'd had to agree to this addition to her original idea. "Pop the trunk," she ordered their driver.

It was after dark, and there were no other cars in the parking lot. There were lights illuminating a runway where a small jet was prepped for take-off. The muted roar of its engines added a keening background noise to this tense meeting.

The lawyer looked at the handcuffed male lying curled up in the trunk. The prisoner was wearing a hooded sweatshirt and sunglasses, and his ankles were bound as well as his hands. "This is the experimental subject the Patron requested?"

"Yep, he's a vampire, all right," Mia answered. She reached into the trunk and lifted Laurent's upper lip. He didn't oblige her by showing even a hint of fang. "He's drugged to the gills with the stuff I was told to use," she added. "So you don't have to be afraid he's going to bite you."

"The subject has the required blood anomalies the lab is looking for," Colin contributed. "Let's get him loaded, shall we?"

The lawyer looked around as if he was afraid they were going to be overheard. And even though Colin's expression hadn't changed, she knew he wasn't happy with her saying the V word. He certainly hadn't been happy when he'd found out that she been furnished with vampire catching equipment, even though they hadn't used it. The blond in the trunk had flinched a little at the mention of drugs; maybe he was afraid of needles.

The lawyer gently lowered the trunk lid. "Thank you for your assistance," he told Mia. "I will take charge of the subject from this point."

"Just what does that mean?" Mia frowned. "My great-grandfather instructed me to bring him the subject."

"I know nothing of those instructions. Your presence is no longer required."

"Oh, no. That's not how this plays out." This lackey was *not* going to snarl up their plan.

"He's not going anywhere without us," Colin seconded. "We're taking him to the Patron."

"That is not possible," the lawyer answered adamantly.

Mia felt her temper rise. "It's imperative," she snapped.

"You will be well compensated for your services," the lawyer said.

"I don't *need* compensation. I am Henry Garrison's great-granddaughter; this is a family matter. I did this for him, and for a good cause. It's not finished until I know the subject is in his possession. Understood?" If this *idiot* didn't—

"My instructions are explicit. I am to take charge of the subject at the rendezvous point and convey it to the research facility. No mention was made of you"—he glanced at Colin—"or anyone else accompanying me."

Mia's temper flared white-hot.

Get out of my way! she shouted as she glared

at the lawyer. *Just do as you're told and get out of my way!*

Colin took a swift step back, his vision flaring bright white and fading quickly to black, the inside of his head ringing with Mia's telepathic shout. He heard a gasp escape Laurent from inside the trunk.

When Colin's vision returned, he saw the lawyer on his knees in front of Mia with his hands clutching his temples, his features a mask of pain. Mia was still glaring at the man, practically incandescent with fury, and he wouldn't have been surprised if flames suddenly shot out of the tips of her fingers. He's always known her temper could flash, but he'd never known it could burn.

He rushed to his bondmate's side and snagged her around the waist, turning her to face him. "Calm down. Focus it," he commanded when she didn't take her gaze off the mortal.

Colin's touch steadied Mia, made everything solid again. He brought the ground back under her feet, put the sky back over her head. His voice brought her back from a dangerous edge. The world had gone away for a moment, leaving only her will. She'd held it like lightning in her hands, and she'd used it like a weapon.

She blinked now, and night air laced with jet fuel and desert dust rushed into her lungs. She coughed, shook her head, and told the man on the ground, "Get out of here."

He sprinted to his car and was gone within seconds, tires screeching as he fled the airport.

Mia collapsed against Colin. "That was me," she said, bewildered. "I did that." Feeling like a lost child, she looked at him for help. "What did I do?"

He held her and explained, "Telepathy. Very strong telepathy."

She rested her forehead on his shoulder and breathed in his scent, starting to feel dizzy. When she looked at Colin again, his face was slightly out of focus. "Domini said I had a psychic gift. That sometime it would just explode."

He nodded. "That was quite an explosion." He touched her cheek with the back of his hand. "It's your gift, and your curse."

She smiled, but it took an effort. She felt exhausted. "Like Spiderman?"

"With great power comes great responsibility," Laurent's muffled voice came from the trunk.

Mia looked toward the car. "We'd better—"

"Not yet." Colin held her tighter. "Wait for it."

"For wha—"

The pain hit like a star going nova inside her head, driving her down into merciful darkness. She thought she heard Colin say, "That's what," just as the darkness closed over her.

Chapter Twenty-four

"Is she still out?" Laurent asked.

Colin glanced across the seating area of the plane's luxurious cabin. The other Prime was buckled into a plush chair opposite the couch where he was seated with Mia. She was lying with her knees drawn up and her head resting in his lap. The pilots were behind the closed cockpit door, and there was no one else on board.

He'd been gazing at her worriedly for a long time, running his fingers through her dark curls. Until Laurent spoke, he'd only been aware of the silky texture of her hair and the muted roar of the jet engines as they flew northeast.

And worry. He was very much aware of aching, desperate worry.

"Is she going to be all right?" Laurent asked.

Fear knotted in Colin's gut, and a hint of

primal jealousy began to creep into his emotions. "Why would you care?"

Laurent raised his cuffed hands dismissively. "Oh, please. You have nothing to worry about from me on her account."

"You came after her," Colin reminded Laurent.

"That was just business. She's too dangerous for my taste, my friend." He tilted his head to one side, studying Colin. "You do know that she's dangerous, right?"

Colin looked back at Mia with pride. "We like them dangerous."

"Dangerous females are liabilities. Dangerous mortal women are even more dangerous. Mortal women with psychic gifts—that's the world turned inside out, upside down, and really, really sick, my friend. You *are* going to ditch her once we're inside the old man's place, right? Or at least put a collar and leash on her, if you plan on keeping her."

"I'm keeping her," Colin growled.

"I know you've been forced into that, and I know you don't like it. You can't trust her, and she's taking us into a lion's den. You better keep an eye on her, and you better keep her under control. If you're going to be her keeper, take a lesson from how we Tribe Primes handle our mortal women."

It would have been tempting to get up and hit the Manticore Prime, but no Clan Prime would strike a helpless prisoner. Laurent probably knew that, and so felt he could say whatever he wanted with impunity. And he seemed genuinely disturbed by Mia's gifts, which amused Colin. But Colin also found the Manticore's attitude very disturbing.

"And how is it you treat your mortal women?"

Laurent heard the danger in Colin's tone, and backed down a bit. He shrugged. "They make nice pets, I'm told. I wouldn't want to keep one, myself. A night and a bite with as many pretty ones as I can score, that's how I relate to the mortal herd."

Laurent's words made Colin squirm. It was like looking into a mirror and seeing a warped reflection. He was no different than a Tribe bastard, when it came down to what was really important. A strong shudder ran through him, and he tasted bile.

Laurent laughed softly. "I see that you know exactly how I feel."

"I knew I should have put a gag on you," Colin said.

The Manticore frowned and rattled the cuffs. They both knew that he could pull them apart any time he wanted, but Laurent was willing to stay in his role as vampire prisoner for the sake of his tribe's agenda.

Perhaps he had some honor, after all. No—even though some of the tribes had been forced into less vicious behavior in the last century, the Manticore were not among that group. Laurent's actions were motivated by greed, and probably fear of his pack leader.

"Justinian trusts you to do the job, does he?" he asked.

Laurent laughed softly. "Justinian would never be fool enough to trust anyone completely." He nodded toward Mia. "Unlike some people I know. When she turns on you, remember that I told you so."

This conversation was going nowhere. Besides, Mia was beginning to stir to consciousness, and the plane was beginning its descent.

"Hello," he said when Mia lifted her head. She groaned, and he helped her sit up very slowly. Her skin was still a little cool to the touch, and there were dark circles under her eyes. "How do you feel?"

Mia put her hands over her face and mumbled, "Head. Hurts."

If it would just fall off and roll gently away, she'd be perfectly happy. Who wanted a head, when it felt like this?

Colin put a comforting arm around her shoulders. "Do you feel kind of blank? Like the inside of your mind is stuffed up? Mental congestion?"

"Yeah."

"Good."

She managed to turn her head just far enough to give Colin a scathing look. "Good?"

"That means you didn't suffer any permanent brain damage, and you'll be better soon."

Ahh, soon—good. Then, "*Brain* damage?"

She heard nearby laughter, and decided that it came from Laurent. Then she realized they were on the plane. They must be on the way to Colorado, though her memories stopped back at the airport parking lot.

Colin patted her arm reassuringly. "You just overloaded a few psychic circuits with your tantrum. With a little rest and a lot of training, you'll be fine."

"You've done the same thing," she concluded.

"When I was a kid, yeah."

Mia didn't like the implication that he considered her psychic gifts somewhere in the juvenile range. Then again, she had a raging headache, so she couldn't objectively conclude if he was being insulting, or if she was just cranky from the pain.

"Is the plane landing?" she asked.

"Yeah. Looks like you woke up just in time."

Just in time? She scrubbed her hands across her face. Just in time for—

Oh, yeah, she had a role to play.

Mia sat up straight and disengaged herself from Colin's embrace. She noticed that Colin didn't try to stop her. In fact, when she glanced at him, he'd put on the distant persona once more. She did her best to look cool, calm, and competent, even with a raging headache and worries about whether this was the right thing to do. And whether she and Colin would ever—

"Heads up," Laurent announced from across the aisle. "We're going wheels down."

"What are you doing here?" Henry Garrison asked Mia. He then pointed a bony finger at Colin. "Who is he? How did you get in here?"

The old boy wasn't happy. But then, Colin doubted that Garrison was ever happy about anything, maybe just less annoyed from time to time. There was a sour anger in him that permeated everything around him. While the room was large and well lit, Colin had the sense of being trapped in a small, dark space with a hungry rat.

He didn't know whether to feel sorry for Mia, that this was her eldest living relative, or worried about the flawed genetics of his future offspring.

He had only seen Garrison at a distance the night he'd helped destroy the research facility, but Colin recognized the thin old mortal, though not the pair of unmoving bodyguards who stood watch behind him. They hadn't been among the mercenaries who'd hustled the Patron onto the airplane he'd escaped on.

There was a wide desk between the old man and where Colin and Mia stood. The only thing on the desk was an open laptop computer. Its matte silver case stood out in stark contrast to the ornate wooden desk, gilt-framed floral prints on the walls, Oriental carpet, and dark velvet wing chairs that made up the room's furnishings.

Somehow, Colin didn't think the Patron was the sort for Victorian decor. This suggested that Garrison had moved in hastily, taking over the remote old mansion sight unseen, and hadn't had the time to make many changes. So hopefully the security system wasn't up to modern standards yet, either. Every little weakness would help in shutting the Patron's operation down permanently this time.

Colin had taken careful note of every step of their movement into the heart of Garrison's compound. Security was tight, but there were obvious weaknesses. The small airport where they'd landed was several miles away from the site, which lessened the Patron's chance of easy escape. This place wasn't as isolated as the facility in Arizona had been, either. There was a perimeter fence and guards at the entrance, but this was no fortified camp. And there was only this one building, though it was huge. When they'd come in, Laurent had been taken down a staircase off the main hall. Colin guessed that the Manticore Prime was now locked in a basement room.

He and Mia had been brought up a sweeping staircase with an ornately carved balustrade to this room at the end of a long hall. A heavy door had been shut behind them, and they'd come face to face with the querulous Henry Garrison.

"Well?" Garrison demanded when he wasn't answered immediately.

Colin and Mia were standing side by side, like kids called into an angry principal's office, but they weren't touching. And Mia didn't look at him when she took a step forward.

"You asked me to bring you a specimen."

Garrison waved her words away impatiently. "I changed that plan. Weren't you informed?"

"I changed it back."

Colin almost smiled. His Mia was not one to be intimidated; he looked forward to watching the old man try to put her in her place.

Instead, the old mortal smiled. It was a thin, grudging, brief movement of his lips, but a spark of real humor lit his cold eyes for a moment. "Apparently you inherited some of my strong will," he told his great-granddaughter.

"I don't know if it comes from you or not," was her answer. "We don't know each other, but we do have a common cause." She gestured at Colin. "We have Mr. Faveau's organization in common, as well."

The name Faveau had been chosen at Tony Crowe's suggestion, Tony being the mortal vampire hunter expert. The Faveau were a family that still hunted, had always hunted, and the name would be known to someone who had grown up in the hunter society of the last century.

"Faveau?" Garrison spared Colin a long, searching look. "You don't look like a Faveau."

"You haven't seen a Faveau in three generations," Colin answered coolly. "We don't all marry our hunter cousins these days. Times have changed, Mr. Garrison. It's time that hunting methods change, as well."

Garrison looked back at Mia. "Why have you brought him here?"

"I wasn't as prepared to capture a vampire on my own as you and I assumed. I needed help." She took a deep breath before she admitted, "I would have gotten killed if the hunters hadn't rescued me. I owe—"

Garrison cut her off. "What you owe them is hardly my concern."

"They want to help," Mia told him, "and they have skills to offer."

"Ms. Luchese told us about your research project," Colin said. "We propose an alliance. We have information to exchange; we've been studying samples of the vampire daylight drugs we've managed to obtain from their clinic in Los Angeles."

That got Garrison's attention. He steepled his fingers, trying not to show any excitement, but Colin could tell that the old mortal's hands were shaking a little.

"Oh, really," Garrison murmured. "You have samples, data?"

"Yes. But we don't have the resources and facilities that Ms. Luchese tells us you do. We have similar goals, Mr. Garrison. We should work together. We even brought you a captured subject as a goodwill gift."

The old man sat back in his high-backed leather chair, and thought for a while. "This could prove productive," he said at last. "The data I'd been gathering for years was recently destroyed. I've disliked the idea of starting over."

"Then let us combine our research," Colin proposed. "The results could put an end to the parasites that prey on humanity, forever."

Mia gave him a brief glance that said he'd gone a bit over the top with this last statement, and Colin agreed with her. But Garrison didn't take any note of the melodramatics.

"I'll think about it," he said. "I'll definitely think about it. We'll talk again. It's late now." He looked at Mia and said, "Go to bed, child."

Colin wondered if the old man meant for his gruff tone to sound grandfatherly.

"Show these two to guest rooms," the Patron ordered one of his guards. "You did well, Caramia," he said as the guard led them toward the door.

Much to Colin's surprise, Mia flashed the old man a shy, delighted smile before stepping out into the hall.

"Thanks, Grandpa," she said.

Chapter Twenty-five

Thanks, Grandpa, Colin repeated over and over with growing alarm as he paced from one side of the third-story bedroom to the other. *Thanks, Grandpa?*

He so disliked being away from Mia. Disliked? Hell, he was growing close to frantic. Bondmate crap, he told himself, tempting him to be unprofessional. He had to stay on the program, follow the procedure they'd set up. So far they hadn't encountered any contingencies they hadn't planned for.

Except—*Thanks, Grandpa.*

What had she meant by that? Was her Garrison blood kicking in to lead her to the dark side?

It didn't help that he couldn't feel her thoughts at the moment. He was aware of where she was, by the blood connection between them. He knew her scent on the air, and the sweet surge of her heartbeat from every other mortal's in the building. But he didn't feel the essence of *her*, and he missed it.

He knew she'd be fine in a little while, that the numbness would wear off. But in the meantime, the separation made him realize just how much a part of him she'd become.

And it wasn't even the horniness that bothered him the most. Oh, he hungered for the touch and taste and responses of her body, as he always did. But he missed *her*. Her voice, her laughter, the conversations they'd been having, in between fights.

And it seemed like the arguments were growing farther apart, the conversations closer. He missed talking to Mia. There was so much about her he didn't yet know, despite the psychic and physical bond between them.

For example, what did she mean by *Thanks, Grandpa*?

The words grated on his senses, set off warning bells of paranoia. Suspicion.

He should have gagged Laurent.

And what about Laurent? Colin looked at his watch. Had the Manticore broken out of his cell yet? Even though he was only a Tribe Prime, Laurent was still Prime. He could take care of himself.

But Mia was only mortal. And as tough and resourceful as she was, it was his duty as Prime, and his right as her bondmate, to be her protector.

Bondmate.

For the first time, Colin smiled. He knew it was a sloppy, sentimental smile, and was glad he was alone as the unfamiliar romantic feeling came over him. This was no time for him to show vulnerability; he had a job to do.

Speaking of which, this had gone on long enough to give Laurent time to escape and to destroy any new research material down in the labs. Colin's job was to make Garrison forget about vampires; Mia's was to retrieve the laptop to give to the Manticores. Then they were going to leave. It was a simple, nonviolent, gentle, peace-loving—stupid!—plan. Colin didn't believe for a minute that it would go down so easily, and he was sure Laurent didn't, either. But Matri Serisa had approved it.

Unfortunately, she was not a war matri like his own clan's legendary Lady Anjelica, who had directed engagements against mortal Purist hunters and Tribe renegades. There was even a rumor that Anjelica had fought Nazis in the French resistance, though Clan females weren't supposed to put their precious selves in harm's way.

He bet Anjelica would have authorized the use

of deadly force if necessary. But Serisa was the one who approved the op. Fortunately, Serisa's bondmate Barak was a war leader, and more practical. He understood the need for having a Plan B.

Right now they were still on track with Plan A, but being separated for any length of time was not part of the plan.

Colin paced some more, and after about five minutes, he decided that he'd had enough. He was going to find Mia.

He listened at the door for a moment, and detected the heartbeat and breathing of a guard posted in the hallway. No need to go through the mortal if he didn't have to.

He crossed to the room's large window. He was three stories up at the rear of the mansion, which was perched at the edge of a cliff. Not only did this provide a spectacular view, it afforded a natural security measure. There'd be a lot more than three stories to fall if you tried to get out the window. Which he intended to. The walls were brick, which an experienced rock climber like himself could scale. Especially an experienced rock climber who came equipped with long, strong claws.

Mia was one floor below and to his right, on the same side of the house. It was late on a cloudy night, but Colin also had excellent night vision. He smiled. This was going to be fun.

Thanks, Grandpa. What on earth had she meant by that?

Mia sat on the heavily carved Victorian bed and looked at the white lace canopy that arched above her head. The room was all pink and white and girly. She was getting really sick of being tucked away in luxurious cells, to be brought out when other people were ready to make pronouncements and decisions.

She was also thoroughly confused by her own behavior. Her hands were clenched tightly together, her stomach was full of acid-winged butterflies, and the headache that had plagued her since she mind-zapped the lawyer was still throbbing against her temples. Frankly, she was a wreck. She needed action, and she wanted Colin. Though she thought he was pissed at her, from the look he'd given her at her *Thanks, Grandpa.*

Colin probably thought she was on the Patron's side. Maybe she was a better actress than she thought, and she'd been really deeply into the moment. Or maybe there was some residual sympathy for the old man's cause lurking somewhere inside her.

Maybe the old man was the one telling the truth, and all the others were the ones lying to her.

She smiled at this thought, and relaxed a little. *Oh, yeah, every vampire I've met has been part of a vast conspiracy to convince me that my opinion of them is the most important thing in the world.* Mia shook her head. *And to think I pointed out to Colin that everything isn't always about him.*

Maybe they were bonded because they were a lot alike. She hoped they were alike in the good ways as well as the egotistical bad ones. Or maybe it was just the sex—she ached for him at the thought.

At the same instant, something tapped on glass behind her. Mia jumped to her feet and whirled toward the room's window. She almost screamed when she saw an upside down face grinning at her wildly through the lace curtain.

She rushed to the window, pulled back the curtain, and lifted the window. There was no ledge. Colin's hands were braced on either side of the window frame, and the rest of his body was held up like a gymnast's at the top of a vault. The thought of the drop he was hanging above terrified her.

"For crying out loud," she whispered fiercely to the vampire clinging head over heels to the outside wall. "You look like a scene from a Dracula movie."

His maniacal expression turned to surprise. "I do?" He laughed softly. "I hadn't thought about that."

She glanced toward the door, where there was a guard posted, as he swung himself into the room. As soon as his feet hit the floor, Mia grabbed him in a tight embrace, her heart hammering in her chest. "You could have been killed!"

"No way. That was easier than rock climbing."

He sounded way too smug, and far too pleased at her getting all huggy on him. Now, wasn't that just like Colin? Which was just the way she liked him, God help her.

She loosened her hold to tug his head down to hers. His hair was silk against her hands, and the touch of his skin overwhelmed her. She kissed him, all her tension fueling her hunger. He cupped her rear and pulled her against him, and their hips ground together in quick mutual arousal.

Colin just wanted to get Mia on the bed, get her under him, get inside her, and feel his cock tightly surrounded by all the soft, yielding heat tha—

"Whoa, whoa, whoa," he said. He let her go

as if he'd been burned. He *was* burning up, on the edge of losing his mind to his desire for her.

"Whoa what?" Mia asked, staring at him with a stricken look in her eyes. Her desire was a perfume surrounding her, calling to him.

Colin took another step back, shaking his head, trying to get his arousal under control. "Not now," he whispered, motioning toward the door.

Mia closed her eyes. She was trembling. He watched her helplessly while she got herself under control. And he kept his hands behind his back, because just looking at her was almost too tempting.

When Mia opened her eyes, there was anger in them.

He desperately wanted to calm her, comfort her—find out what was pissing her off.

He said, "Laurent's escape is overdue. We have to do something."

"Are you sure he's still locked up?"

Colin nodded, but before he could say anything, the door opened.

Four of the guards entered, all carrying guns. Garrison came in after them with an aide at his side. The old man leaned on a cane. Colin was aware that there were other armed men out in the hall.

He could take them out if he had to, but—

"Grandpa!" Mia shouted, and rushed forward.

Weapons were raised, but she ignored them, though she stopped short of touching the Patron.

"I'm so glad you're here!" She pointed at Colin. "He wants me to help him steal your data. The hunters don't really trust you, and I didn't ask for their help catching the vampire. When they surrounded your people at the airport, I couldn't think of a way out of bringing him here. And then he showed up in here and told me he wasn't going to wait for you to make a decision—"

Garrison cut her off. "You are a very talkative young woman."

"I guess that doesn't run in the family," Colin said, which focused Garrison's attention on him. Colin glared at Mia. "How did you manage to call for help? And why? Is blood so much more important than the cause?"

She whirled to face him. "You have no right to force the issue. I won't let you sabotage my grandfather's work."

"Blood is what it is all about, Faveau," Garrison spoke up. "Finding out what's in their blood that makes them what they are. It's a pity you chose not to wait for my decision. I sent for you to tell you that I would work with your people."

"You can't trust them," Mia put in.

"So it seems."

"But you still need their data."

"You won't get any help from us now," Colin said.

"Which is why you won't get out of here alive," Garrison calmly responded. "If we have no mutual need—"

"But there *is* someone that needs him." Mia smiled slowly, and her expression was diabolical enough to make Colin nervous. "The vampire. Why don't you put the vampire hunter in with the vampire for a while? If the creature's hungry . . . I suspect Mr. Faveau would rather share his data than become snack food for the thing he hunts."

"Bitch," Colin said to her, then told Garrison, "You can't torture what you want out of me."

The old man shrugged one frail shoulder. "But there's no harm in trying. Dump him in with the creature," he told his guards.

As he was led out the doorway, Colin heard Garrison say, "Caramia, child, you are an asset to the family after all. Come and join me for a drink."

Chapter Twenty-six

The pain was so bad, Laurent could barely stand it. The blinding bright lights far overhead burned his eyes, even though they were closed. The temperature was cranked up to the point that it nearly scalded his skin, and they'd stripped him down to his underwear so there was a lot of skin to burn. But the restraints were the worst, fastening his arms behind his back. The searing agony around his wrists was so great that he'd gnaw his hands off to get free of the pain, if he could only get to them.

Lying on the floor, curled up in a ball and concentrating hard on trying not to scream, he almost didn't hear the door open. Someone was shoved inside, and the door closed again before he could gather the strength to lift his head, let alone make a lunge for freedom.

When he did manage to lift his head and pry

his eyes open, it took several tortured moments for his gaze to travel up a long, lean body dressed in black and finally reach the face of the new-comer.

"Oh, it's you," he managed to croak out.

Colin Foxe squatted beside him. Squinting in the hideous light, he looked Laurent over. "What happened to you?"

"I don't do drugs," Laurent rasped out.

He wasn't sure if he was more furious at the Clan vampire who was merely inconvenienced by the things that were killing him, or at the Tribe alphas who forbade the use of the elixirs that would keep away this pain. Mostly, he just wanted the pain to go away. He wanted it to go away so badly that he couldn't stop the moan that escaped him. But this one sound of weak-ness was the closest he'd come to begging.

Foxe reached out and turned Laurent onto his stomach. "Damn. They put silver on you."

"I—noticed."

Laurent could have broken the steel hand-cuffs he'd worn when he entered the cell. But before he had the chance, someone had picked up an ampule from a selection on a cart and stuck a needle into his neck. When he woke he was alone, stripped, and silver bound his wrists. Silver was a soft metal, and even a mortal female could twist off the cuffs that hooked his arms together. But the burning agony of silver against his skin paralyzed him and made the task impossible.

Colin saw that Laurent's skin was badly burned. The daylight drugs only offered him partial protection from silver burns, so he pulled off his shirt and wrapped it around his hands before touching the manacles. Even with the protection of layers of cotton, Colin's skin grew uncomfortably warm before he was able to pull the soft metal apart. It took a few more moments to pry Laurent's wrists out of the cuffs. Once they dropped to the floor, Colin stood and kicked them aside.

Colin didn't offer to help Laurent up, but turned his back to give the other Prime privacy to get himself together. A couple of minutes passed before he heard Laurent take a deep breath and slowly rise to his feet.

Colin turned back and said, "We wondered why you were late."

"The bastards were tricky." He gave Colin a very annoyed once-over. "Now we're locked up together. What happened? Did the girl turn you in, too?"

"Yes."

Despite the lines of pain that still marred his

face, Laurent managed to look smug. "Didn't I warn you not to trust her?"

Colin picked up his shirt and put it on before saying, "You warned me." He gave the other Prime a warning look. "And if she wasn't so soft-hearted, I wouldn't be here to save your ass."

"Save my—she betrayed you, dude!"

"No, she betrayed the guy I'm pretending to be. When I told her that you might be in trouble, she managed to get the old man to toss a vampire hunter in with a vampire. Not bad for a spur-of-the-moment Plan B. The woman has promise, and I can't wait to tell her so." He smiled fondly, as though this was a revelation to him.

All Laurent wanted was to get out of here. "Fine," he told the besotted fool. "All praise to your lady, and other flowery Clan crap." He gestured toward the locked door. "What's next?"

"Back to Plan A. Only now we bust out and destroy all the data we can find."

Right, he'd been supposed to destroy computer disks and stuff like that. Who cared? What mattered was the payday—not that the noble, and rich, Clan boy was concerned with that.

"Lead on," he said.

Colin crossed to the door and dug his claws into the lock plate. While the Clan Prime pried out the lock, Laurent went to the table, picked up one of the filled syringes, and moved close to Colin.

"How's it coming?"

After a moment Colin said, "Done."

Laurent didn't know what was in the syringe, but he had no qualms about sticking it into Colin's shoulder and pressing the plunger. Being a prisoner had taken up too much of the night, and he needed a head start to the premises. Justinian had ordered him to bring back Garrison's wealth, and he wasn't ready to defy the pack leader's wishes yet.

"Sorry," he told Colin as the other vampire fell heavily onto the floor. "But I've got to put my own Plan B in motion."

Mia hoped Colin wasn't mad at her. After all, she'd done the right thing, and he had gone along with it. She wished she could feel him; then she wouldn't be so confused and worried.

The headache was finally gone, so maybe she'd have the full use of her abilities back soon. Being deprived of these brand-new senses made her more aware of them, made her *want* them. They completed her, enhancing her connection to Colin.

She hated that she didn't know where he was right now. She'd thrown him into trouble, and she'd just have to trust him to get out. And it came down to who you trusted, didn't it? Just like Domini said. Colin was easy to get pissed off at, but impossible not to trust when push came to shove. Did he realize she knew that, though?

She followed her great-grandfather down the corridor to a small elevator with an ornate brass gate. A pair of his guards followed them closely.

Mia tried hard to keep her mind on the moment, but thoughts of Colin kept rolling around her head.

Did he know she wasn't angry with him for pulling away from her just before the bad guys showed up? She knew he'd felt her emotion, but she hadn't had time to explain that she was annoyed with herself.

She had no business tempting him—them—in the middle of a dangerous situation. She'd gotten thrown into all this action without any training, and now she had to deal with this bonding thing and—

She took a deep breath as they stepped into the narrow elevator cage. Mia squeezed in first, and the old man followed, standing with his back to her. She still didn't want anything to happen to the old man, but she was more convinced than ever that he was dangerous and had to be neutralized.

There wasn't any room for the bodyguards, so they hurried down the stairs so they'd be waiting on the first floor when the elevator finished its slow descent.

"How did he get into your room?"

The old man's voice had a cricket rasp to it, and he was leaning heavily on his cane. But there was no doubting the strength of his will or the sharpness of his mind.

"How did you know he was in my room?" she answered. When he didn't reply immediately, she let the subject go, and guessed, "You don't have long to live, do you?"

"No mortal does." He sighed and turned his head to look at her. "I have very little time, and the vampires cheated me out of much of it a few months ago. Now I must rush to rebuild what was lost. Perhaps I could have used your help sooner."

Mia could barely keep her revulsion in check. It sickened her to realize how much this man had destroyed and abandoned in his quest for eternal life. Had he actually lived the life he'd been given? Did he know what he'd given up, or care at all?

"You're just evil, aren't you, Grandpa?"

The elevator stopped as she asked her question, and the door slid smoothly open to reveal three people waiting for them. The guards were lying at the bottom of the stairs, and the scent of blood filled the air.

Mia's emotions spiked with terror as she recognized the tall male who stepped forward, smiling coldly. He held a hand out. "Come with me," Justinian said. "I'll teach you about evil."

I'm getting good at this, Laurent thought as he ripped another door off its hinges.

The action not only got him into the locked rooms on the third floor, but also alleviated his growing frustration.

There had been a guard at either end of the hall when Laurent came dashing up the stairs, but he'd moved on them with speed no mortal could match. Disarming and disabling them had helped him work through his annoyance at his treatment.

Once the guards were out of the way, he began his hunt. Recovering the Manticore's stolen fortune was all he'd signed on for.

He didn't give a damn about the traditional revenge aspect of the scenario; he didn't care about this mad Patron's evil experiments.

If the old guy could find the secret of immortality for mortals, it might threaten vampire existence, but vampires had been threatened

throughout history. Laurent didn't see any reason why they wouldn't survive the menace from
the Patron—as long as he wasn't the one being
personally experimented on.

Besides, if the Patron managed to find his
magic live-forever potion, think how much
Garrison's company's stock would be worth.
Laurent rather liked the idea of the Manticores
taking control of Garrison's holdings. It would
satisfy their right to reimbursement, and solve
Justinian's need for revenge. Everybody would
profit. Maybe he could talk Justinian into it.

But first, he had to find Garrison's computer.
The mortal woman was right that the laptop
likely held all the financial information they
needed.

The room he stepped into this time had the
look of an office. He might finally be getting
somewhere.

First he ripped apart the desk and found nothing. That was fun, but then he got himself under
control and began a more methodical search of
the room. It didn't take him long to find the safe
tucked behind a large portrait of a very ugly
woman. The gleaming steel door of the safe was
set flush against the wall. Brute strength wasn't
going to do any good here, but what was the use
of having extremely fine hearing if one couldn't

use it to listen for the correct combination while carefully spinning the tumblers? He pressed his head against the cool steel and got to work.

Patience, he told himself. Patience.

To his delighted surprise, it didn't take long at all to open the door. He was even more delighted to find a small leather computer case resting inside the safe.

"All right!" he congratulated himself, and reached for the case.

His elation died the moment he had the computer in his grasp.

They were here, earlier than he'd expected or wanted. He'd been concentrating too hard to notice their arrival, but he was acutely aware of the pack's presence now. Most were concentrated in one area of the house, but there were others scattered around the grounds. So Justinian had brought the whole pack with him. That hadn't been the plan.

It sent a chill up his spine; even though he was with them, he wasn't one of them. Laurent held Justinian's triumph in his hands, and that should count for something. But his fellow Tribe Primes were so unpredictable, especially in large groups, where they egged each other on.

He turned slowly away from the safe. It was easy enough to follow the Manticore's mental signature down the flights of stairs to the first floor.

The first thing Laurent noticed when he found the pack was that there were over a dozen Primes scattered around the ballroom. The place was so big, even a dozen vampires didn't take up much of the space. There was a crystal chandelier blazing overhead, but it didn't throw that much light into the room. A huge, empty fireplace and several groupings of heavy old furniture made up the rest of the room. No windows, Laurent noted; that was always a plus in a building designed for mortal inhabitants.

"And speaking of mortal inhabitants," he murmured, spotting the pair surrounded by Primes in one of the seating areas.

Justinian and Belisarius were standing in front of them, and another pair of Primes were poised behind the couch. One had his hands on the old man's bony shoulders. The other had a hand twisted in the female's short curls.

"Oh, hell." Laurent rushed forward, but was stopped by a stern look from Justinian. Laurent held up the leather case in his hand. "I have what we came for. Let's get out of here."

"I'm not done here." Justinian looked back at the prisoners. "The Garrisons have to pay."

"What are you going to do? Mind-rape them

for information? You don't need to do that. We have what rightfully belongs to the Manticores. We can leave."

"What use is a black bag?" Belisarius sneered. "All his money couldn't fit in that."

"It's not the bag that's important, but the data in the computer inside it. You do know what a computer is, right?" Laurent knew that sarcasm was dangerous, but he just couldn't help himself.

"Garrison's data will be password-protected," Belisarius said to Justinian. "I can rip those passwords from his mind if you wish."

Okay, so Belisarius wasn't completely ignorant, just stupid and brutal. And the old man probably deserved what he got.

Probably? Laurent shook his head in disgust at this softness. There must've been wimp juice in the drink he'd had at the Clan house.

"Do what you want with the old man—" he began.

"I will," Justinian purred.

"But remember that the Garrison female also belongs to the Reynard Prime. Hurt her, and you risk a war with the Clans."

"He's afraid of the Clans," Belisarius sneered.

"We've been through this before," Laurent said with a sigh.

He gave up and stepped back. He knew from

the glittering edge to Justinian's emotions, the look of greedy anticipation on Belisarius's face, and the general eagerness for blood sport pulsing in the psychic atmosphere that the time of reasonableness had past.

"You guys just can't hold it together, can you?"

Of course, Laurent was ignored.

Justinian concentrated on Garrison. "Will you trade the passwords for the female's life? Remember that she is your only chance at immortality, old man. So will you trade your empire for something more important?'

Garrison looked steadily at Justinian, and replied calmly, "Of course not."

The female didn't look surprised.

Justinian looked delighted. "We'll see." He told Belisarius, "Make her scream."

Chapter Twenty-seven

Colin was lost in thick, clinging fog that enwrapped him so he couldn't see or taste or feel where his body ended and the fog began. He was alone. Completely alone. And something was terribly, terribly wrong. The fog allowed him fear, and pain that boiled up from his soul. There was so much pain—in his heart, in his head, permeating his body, blocking out any chance of joy or completion or—love.

He was lost, and he'd never love again. Or be loved.

I wish you all the time in the world to enjoy what you have. Cherish each day.

David Berus's voice rang in his head. Then the Serpentes Prime's hand was on his shoulder. They stood together—

And looked down on a grave.

"No," Colin said. He closed his eyes and turned away. "No!"

Mia was gone. Dead. Lost.

"Isn't that what you wanted?" Laurent asked. "She wasn't worthy of you."

Colin whirled to the Tribe Prime, ready to kill. But Laurent wasn't there. "Liar!" he shouted to the phantom. Yet he knew that the one who lied was himself, about who he wanted and needed. He was an arrogant fool, unworthy of her.

David Berus wasn't to be seen, either.

Colin was alone in the fog, fog that was swiftly turning to fire. Colin didn't care. He burned from the inside out now, aching hunger gnawing at him.

"This is how it feels," Berus said from out of the fire, "to lose what you love."

Colin had a memory of childishly admiring Berus for having survived the loss of his bondmate. Now that admiration turned to compassion.

And to hopelessness.

"I can't live like this," he called to Berus.

"It isn't living."

This was hell. Having Mia ripped from him was hell. Being without her was hell. She was— everything.

"She can't be dead."

"Why not?" Laurent sneered.

"Because."

"Not an answer, Clan boy."

It wasn't any of the Tribe bastard's business. So Colin held the all-important words inside, speaking only to his empty soul.

Because I never had the chance to tell her how much I love her, Colin thought.

Pain ripped through the left side of Colin's chest, and a shout of pure fury stabbed into his mind. His eyes flashed open in shock, and he was momentarily blinded by the light of the bright, bright room.

"Touch me there again, and I'll rip your heart out!"

Colin sat up so fast that he cracked the back of his head on the wall he'd been slumped against. Mia's fury and fear ripped through the fiery fog and brought him fully awake.

Mia!

Colin!

She was alive! He was out of hell!

Colin! Help!

She needed him—and it was her fierce energy that brought him back to life.

"Mia!" he shouted, and jumped to his feet.

At least he tried, but for a moment all he could do was flail helplessly on the cell floor. What the hell was the matter with—

Laurent. A jab of pain. Then he was dizzy and down. He'd been drugged by the Manticore. He'd been lying here hallucinating while his woman needed him.

Move, he told himself. *Carefully. Steadily.* He took slow, deep breaths. Got his legs under him. He stood, and waited until he was certain he could keep standing.

While he did all this, he fought to keep from shaking with fury and shared pain as Mia's torture played out in his mind.

A few seconds was all it took to be sure he could function, but those seconds brought him a lifetime of anxiety before he flew out the door.

She wasn't screaming enough to suit Belisarius, and Laurent wished she would—then maybe Belisarius wouldn't hurt her so much.

Belisarius was having way too good a time. His actions excited the others, who shared laughter and encouragement, and made bets about how long the mortal would last.

Justinian stood back with his arms crossed, watching his beta Prime torture a helpless woman like a proud papa watching his boy at a track meet.

Laurent stayed still and silent in the shadows, and wished it would stop.

The old man didn't seem to be paying attention at all.

When Belisarius lifted a hand with claws fully extended, Laurent looked away. So he was the only one who saw the streak coming through the open doorway.

Foxe was awake and coming to the rescue—of course. Surely he was aware that there was a pack of excited, bloodthirsty Primes surrounding the object of his noble desires?

And Laurent was the only Prime in the room aware of the approaching threat. Not only did Foxe move fast, his psychic shielding was incredibly strong. That made his approach doubly silent and dangerous.

Laurent supposed it was his duty to shout out a warning to his Manticore brethren—but they ought to have been on guard in the first place, he decided. So he stepped even farther into the shadows, and waited to see what would happen.

Strength of numbers or purity of heart? He certainly didn't care to place a bet.

One moment, Mia was only aware of the sharp claws arcing down toward her face. The next thing she saw was a black streak rocketing toward her. Then Colin put himself between her and her tormentor.

Colin's attack forced the other vampire to drop his tight hold on her upper arm. Mia stumbled back and fell to her knees. Though she was bruised and scared, the elation of having her bondmate defend her overrode everything else.

She wanted to help Colin, but the fighters were moving so quickly she could barely see more than flashing fangs, raking claws, and fiercely straining muscles.

She looked around and saw the other vampires moving in, circling the fight, waiting to see how Colin's battle with their comrade played out before they joined the attack. Her heart sank at the realization that her man didn't have a chance. Even if he defeated the one he was fighting, the others would be all over him.

Mia scrubbed a hand across her face. *Think!* She'd gotten Colin into this deadly situation—how was she going to help get him out of it? Her thoughts raced. Silver, garlic, hawthorn, sunlight, high-caliber bullets, mortar rounds, C4, napalm, nuclear radiation, Stinger missiles— *Think, woman! What's at hand?* There must be an arsenal of weapons against vampires in this place. All she had to do was get through the line of vampires and find something she could use.

Colin threw Belisarius onto a low table, and the old furniture was crushed beneath the impact. Wood splintered, and the two Primes scrambled for sharply pointed shards to use as stakes.

"Dust him, Colin!" Mia shouted encouragement.

The fighters lunged closer and she had to scramble backward onto the couch to get out of Colin's way. She kicked at Belisarius in passing. Her foot connected with his jaw, and Belisarius turned his head.

Colin drove his wood splinter into the side of the other Prime's neck. Blood spurted, and Belisarius howled. Then Colin's fangs sank deep into the other side of Belisarius's throat, and his claws ripped deep into the Manticore's chest.

Mia felt the instant Belisarius died, like a psychic candle suddenly being snuffed out. She had a moment of elation at Colin's survival, but it turned to terror even as Colin sprang to his feet to face the circle of Tribe Primes, Belisarius's blood on his face and hands. Despite Colin's snarling triumph and defiance of the pack, they were still deeply, deeply in trouble.

Mia rose to her feet. She was aware that her great-grandfather slumped sideways when she moved, but she didn't have time for concern for the old man right now. She stood side by side with her bondmate as the pack slowly circled them, eyes glowing, fangs bared.

"Take them apart," Justinian ordered. "Do it slowly."

This was definitely a scene out of her worst nightmare. Only in her nightmares the man she loved wasn't with her. Maybe she was going to die, but at least she wasn't alone.

"What have we got to fight vampires with?" she whispered out of the corner of her mouth.

Colin wiped the blood off his mouth, and his hands on his shirt as he looked beyond the encroaching pack. Then he flexed his fingers and gave her a bright, reassuring smile.

"Personally, I think other vampires are good to fight vampires with," he said.

Then Barak, Tony, Alec, David Barus, and others whose names she didn't know came out of the shadows, encircling the Tribe vampires.

"Back to the original Plan B," Colin said. Then he put himself between her and immediate danger as the fighting started all over again.

Mia took her gaze away from the body on the couch when Tony Crowe came up to her. "Is it over?"

Colin was outside, searching for those who were trying to get away.

"It's all over except for the cover-up," Tony answered.

The fight hadn't gone on for very long, but it had spread all through the house and the estate grounds. Mia hadn't taken part; she'd been giving CPR to her great-grandfather. And that had been done out of hopeless duty, because—

"He's gone," Tony said. "No light of soul left at all."

"I know." She also knew that the old man hadn't had a soul for a long time. "I don't know if one of the vampires killed him, or if it was just his time." She rubbed the back of her neck. "I did what I could."

"I'm sure you did."

She supposed he was thinking that Garrison's death left the vampires one less loose end to tie up. She couldn't blame him for feeling that way, but was glad he was too polite to say so.

He took her by the shoulder and turned her away from the couch. "We'll take care of everything. And thank you," he added. "Your plan worked."

Mia gave him a sardonic look. "Which part of my plan involved you and the bad guys showing up?"

"Ah. Those elements were factored in later. We knew we couldn't trust the Manticores to abide by the rules, so we—"

"Didn't follow the rules, either," she contributed. "Not that I mind."

"They followed Laurent, we followed you. Our only surprise was that Justinian's people got here first." He gave an eloquent shrug. "It all worked out. There were mortal casualties," he told her. "I'm sorry, but the Manticores killed two of the guards."

In movies and television shows, no one worried about the spear carriers. She'd hoped to keep very real humans from getting hurt. "It would have been much worse if you hadn't shown up. Did you kill Manticores?"

"A couple of them got away, but most of them surrendered," he answered. "That's almost too bad, because now we have to lock 'em up and reeducate them, and that takes years."

Suddenly a thrill ran through her and Mia turned away, all her senses focusing on the most important thing in the world. Colin had entered the room, and she didn't care about anything else.

He came to her, took her hands, and smiled, but he spoke to Tony first. "It looks like Laurent and Justinian got away."

"We'll keep looking." Tony stepped away.

Colin took her in his arms, and Mia collapsed gratefully into his sheltering embrace. They did nothing but hold each other for a long time.

"Hell of a night," he finally said. Then he held

her out at arm's length. "Are you all right? What can I do to help?"

Mia was incredibly touched by his gentleness and concern. She couldn't answer for a moment, overwhelmed just by looking at him. He was strong, brave—handsome. She'd known all these things, but now she recognized and absorbed how much everything he was, was a part of her.

"As you are a part of me," he told her. "Come on."

He put his arm around her waist, and they went out into the morning light. The breeze was scented with pine, and morning sunlight sparked off snow-covered peaks. Mia took a deep breath. Then Colin kissed her and took her breath away.

"I was so afraid of losing you," he said when they finally came up for air. "Afraid of losing you before we really found each other. I've been a fool and a jerk and a complete—"

"I know." She put her fingers over his lips. "Don't make a speech about it, okay?"

He kissed her palm and she thought she was going to melt. "You deserve a speech."

His earnestness sent joy flooding through her. "Yeah, but it wouldn't match the groveling abasement I've lovingly imagined."

"That's harsh." His eyes sparkled teasingly. "Do I get down on my knees, in your fantasy?"

"Yeah, but not in the apology fantasy." His low, wicked chuckle sent a thrill through Mia. "Just apologize and tell me you love me, and we'll be okay." She held him close.

"I'm sorry."

He ran his hands down her back and looked thoughtfully out at the mountains. For a moment she grew cold with dread. Maybe he wasn't able to say the words.

"I've never told you that I love you, have I, Caramia?" He laughed softly. "Of course, your name says it all. *Cara mia* means 'my love,' doesn't it?"

"Yes."

He rubbed his cheek against hers, and whispered in her ear, "I'm never going to call you anything else. I love you, Caramia."

"And I love you."

"Really?" he asked eagerly. "Since when?"

"You first."

"Probably when you yelled at me for being late to the hostage rescue. I thought it was lust, but the connection went so much deeper. You?" he urged.

"When you showed up at the hospital to see if I was all right."

"I just wanted to get into your pants."

"Yeah, but it was still sweet. And you get

extra points for saving me from Belisarius. I *really* love you for that." She fluttered her eyelashes at him, but she meant it when she said, "I knew you'd come for me, my hero."

"Damn right. You know I'll always be there for you, right?"

"Damn right." She gave Colin her complete and utter trust.

"I was so scared of losing you. The bondmate in danger thing really helped me put things in perspective. You tired, Caramia?"

"Exhausted. And tired of the whole situation. Let's go home."

"To your place," he said. "You've got more room. You're going to have to adjust to being married to a cop. That won't be easy, Caramia."

"It has to be easier than adjusting to being bonded to a vampire."

"I guess."

"And you have to adjust to being married to a vampire hunter."

"What!" He held her out at arm's length again. "No way."

"Yes," she answered. "There are bad guys out there that need policing. It's part of my heritage, and I'm going for it. But properly, officially, with your help and training."

He clearly didn't like it, but he didn't argue.

Mia figured there'd be plenty of time to argue when they got home. Arguing was one of the things they did very well together. They had a long lifetime to do lots of things well together.

He put his arm around her shoulders once more and led her toward the driveway, where they approached a lovely, low-slung red sports car. She didn't know who it belonged to, or if there were keys in it. But she did know that Colin Foxe had every intention of driving away with her in it.

"You know what I'm going to do when we get back to Los Angeles?" he asked as he held the passenger door open for her. "After making love to you for a couple of days?"

"What?"

"Take you to Harry Winston's and buy you a proper wedding ring. Something with lots of diamonds."

"Or rubies," she answered, succumbing to a sudden impulse. "I think I'll let you buy me rubies."

She glanced for the last time at the mansion perched on the mountainside as Colin slid into the driver's seat.

"Let's go home." She smiled at him, and at being with him forever, as they drove away.

POCKET STAR BOOKS
PROUDLY PRESENTS

PRIMAL HEAT

Available in paperback
from Pocket Star Books

Turn the page for a preview of
Primal Heat. . . .

"**Y**our in-laws are scary," Phillipa Eliot told her sister, who was a lovely and not-in-the-least blushing bride.

Phillipa leaned against the terrace railing next to her sister, and took another sip of very good champagne. The hot wind that blew in off the desert didn't bother her. Heck, she was from Phoenix; there was no way Las Vegas could get hotter than home. The dry air did make her thirsty, though; she thought she was on her fifth glass of champagne.

Josephine's eyes went wide. "What do you mean by scary?"

Phillipa looked at the people dancing at the wedding reception in the hotel ballroom. "They make me feel like I've crashed the supermodels' annual ball."

Jo laughed. "Yeah, I know exactly what you mean." Her gaze didn't leave her new husband, who was currently dancing with their mother. "Isn't he—?"

"Large," Phillipa cut in.

"I was going to say cute."

Phillipa laughed. "Of course you were."

She thought that the hulking groom was probably the least handsome man there. Not that the muscular Marcus Cage didn't have enough charm and charisma for three normal males. It seemed to run in the Cage family, and among all their friends. The women were amazingly beautiful, mostly in a dark and mysterious way. And the men—good lord!

They'd been hitting on her since the rehearsal dinner the night before. It had been quite a stimulating experience.

Phillipa took a moment to fan her face. She wasn't sure if it was the champagne, or the mere thought of the men at the reception that was causing the warmth that stirred through her. There was something special about this bunch; after all, she was a cop and used to working around hunky, hard-bodied, macho men. Not only was she used to it, she liked it. But the Cages and their friends had so much going for them in the confident, sexy male department that they were downright daunting.

"It's not that I don't like the Cage clan," Phillipa explained.

"Family," Josephine said. "They're a family, not a clan."

"What difference does that make?"

Jo laughed. "Never mind, and I can't explain anyway. If I did, they'd probably have to kill you. It's a joke between Marc and me," she added quickly.

Phillipa let it go. Far be it from her to try to interpret the private language of newlywed lovebirds, especially after five glasses of champagne.

She looked at her empty glass, and said, "I'm switching to water." One of the groom's hunky relatives was heading their way, and his gaze was fixed on her. "Right now," she added, and left so he'd have to ask her sister to dance instead of her.

The band stopped playing as she skirted the dance floor and she noticed Marc heading for Jo, and Mom heading toward where Dad waited for her. Phillipa smiled, appreciating the devotion of the happy couples. At the same time, she had to fight off a twinge of sadness at being alone herself. She blamed the self-pity on the champagne, because she had no one to blame for breaking up with Patrick but Patrick. You'd think with all the gorgeous men in the place, she'd be more interested in hooking up with one of them.

Maybe I don't want another macho man. Maybe that was why all the groom's male relatives set off alarm bells she couldn't explain.

The band started playing again as she reached the bar.

"Not more Queen," a man said behind her.

The disgust in his voice amused her, and the deep British accent was intriguing. As the band continued with "Another One Bites the Dust," she took the water the bartender handed her, then turned around. She hadn't noticed the man standing behind her before, though she was somehow aware of his presence before he spoke. His hair was wavy and sandy brown, his eyes green and surrounded by laugh lines. He had a lived-in face; a dangerous face.

"I know what you mean," she told him. "If they play 'Fat-Bottomed Girls,' I'm out of here."

"I'll join you," he answered.

"And if they start playing a lot of Def Leppard, Jo will run away screaming."

Phillipa moved away from the crowd surrounding the bar. The newcomer followed after her as she edged around the dance floor on her way back to the terrace.

"Who's Jo, and what's wrong with Def Leppard? I'm a proud son of Sheffield myself," he added.

"Where's that?"

"Northern England. Same hometown as the Lep—?"

"And what do you mean, who's Jo?" Phillipa stopped and confronted him. "You *are* a guest at the Elliot-Cage wedding, aren't you?"

His smile was devastating, showing deep dimples and crinkling the lines around his eyes. "I'm the best man."

Irritation flared over the heat that had been

roused by his smile. "You're Matt Bridger!" she accused. "You very nearly ruined this wedding!"

"It's not my fault my plane was late."

"You were supposed to have arrived yesterday."

He gestured at the boisterous people filling the crowded room. "It doesn't look like I was missed."

"One of my brothers stepped in as best man."

"Then it all turned out all right." He crossed his arms over his wide chest, and moved close to her. "I don't know what you have to be angry about."

"I'm angry on my sister's behalf."

"Why's that?"

"She's Jo Elliot."

"The singer in Def Leppard?"

"The bride!"

Even as she indignantly declared this, Phillipa realized that Matt Bridger was perfectly aware of it, and that he was teasing her.

She stepped closer to him. Suddenly they were toe to toe and nose to nose. He put an arm around her waist, drawing her even closer. She was caught by the masculine heat and scent of him. "You're provoking me on purpose."

The back of his hand brushed across her cheek. "Yes."

Her knees went weak and she almost dropped her glass. She didn't notice where it went when he took it out of her hand.

"Dance with me."

"Yes."

And she never wanted to dance with anyone else.

He drew her onto the dance floor, and they started dancing slowly to the fast music. It was the most natural thing in the world to gaze into this stranger's eyes and press her body against his, soft and hard blending. They didn't share a word while the music played, yet the communication between them was deep and profound. She'd known him forever, been waiting for him forever. It was all too perfect to make any sense.

When the music stopped she would've kept right on dancing, but Matt turned them off the dance floor. Her arms stayed draped around his wide shoulders and her gaze stayed locked with his. His palms pressed against the small of her back, large and warm and possessive.

Despite this intimate closeness, Phillipa tried to regain her sanity.

"We've just met."

"And you're really not that kind of girl."

"What kind of girl?"

"The sort who snuggles up to a stranger the moment they meet. And I'm not that sort of man." He flashed that devastating smile at her again. "Mostly."

"Then why are we—"

"We have more than snuggling in mind."

"Yes, but—"

"I have a theory."

She didn't want to hear his theory. "Kiss me."

Fingers traced across her lips. "Soon."

His touch left her sizzling. This was crazy! She should be embarrassed. Phillipa took a deep breath and made an effort to step away. She managed to move maybe an inch, a small triumph for public decency.

"Like calls to like," he said, pulling her back to him.

She lost interest in decency. "I'm a cop."

"Fancy that." As the music started again, he took her by the hand. The connection was electric. "Come on."

She held back. This was her last chance to stay virtuous. "I don't—"

"Listen."

She did, and laughed. "Oh my God, 'Fat-Bottomed Girls.'"

"You said you'd leave if they played it."

"Left alone with big fat Fanny—she was such a naughty nanny . . ." sang the band.

"Matt Bridger, let's get out of here."

They headed toward the door, but he stopped after a few steps. "One thing, first."

"What?"

"Your name."

"Phillipa Elliot."

At least she wasn't about to fall into reckless abandon with a *total* stranger, now.

He tilted his head and gave her a quick, thorough once-over. What he saw was a tall blond woman in a strapless tea-length teal satin bridesmaid's dress.

"I know, I don't look like a Phillipa," she said. "But who does?"

"Pardon me for saying so, but that is an unfortunate name for a Yank, isn't it?"

"I'm used to it."

"Good. It suits you."

The band started in on the chorus again, and they ran for the door.

They didn't kiss until they were in the elevator, coming together in a rush of heat. His mouth was hard and demanding on hers, and she responded just as fiercely. The way he caressed her made her feel naked despite the satin dress and layers of undergarments. His fingers tracing along her bare shoulders and the back of her neck drove her wild. She knew this was crazy, but she didn't care.

Until she noticed that her skirt was hiked up around one hip and his hand was stroking the inside of her thigh. It felt wonderful.

"We're not exactly private here," she reminded him. "Hotel"—she gasped as his fingers moved higher—"security."

"Room key," was his answer.

He stopped long enough for her to fumble

open her tiny purse, and the doors slid open onto the fourteenth floor just as she pulled out the black plastic key card.

"This is it." She didn't remember pressing the button for her floor, but she hadn't told him where her room was. Odd. At least the room wasn't far from the elevators, and they were there within a few moments.

Inside, he whirled her around onto the bed.

"You make me dizzy," she said as he leaned over her and she looked into his green eyes.

"Only dizzy?"

There was a wicked glint in those eyes, and a world of sensual promise in his slight smile. There was also something dangerous about his deep, slightly rough voice. The sound of it sent a thrill through her.

"Say something else."

He chuckled. "What is it about Yank women and English accents?"

"Don't complain if it helps you get laid," she told him.

He laughed again. "Would this sound seductive in Sheffield?" he asked, doing a very good job of mimicking an American accent.

"Yes. But it's not just your accent that's sexy. You have gorgeous lips," she added. When she traced them with a finger, he nipped it. "And sharp teeth."

"Oh, yes." He kissed her throat.

Her blood raced as warm lips pressed against her tender skin. His hand brushed across the satin covering her breast, sparking the overwhelming desire to have his naked flesh against hers.

A moment later he tugged her to her feet and pulled on the dress's long zipper. As the dress pooled around her feet, his thumb slid slowly down the length of her bare spine. She arched against him.

"Skin on skin, just like you want," he murmured. His lips were close to her ear. Then they were on her throat.

There was a moment of sharp pain, followed by blinding ecstasy. When her mind cleared from the blissful overload, they were back on the bed once more, and he was as naked as she was. She ran her hands across his chest, and appreciating the sight and texture of hard muscles and hot flesh.

"You are so sweet," he told her.

"I'm more than sweet." She pulled his head down and kissed him hard.

"You're also hot," he agreed.

He kissed her gently, on the lips and on the cheek. But she was aware of the edge of ferocity he was holding back. Then his head moved down and his tongue swirled around one hard nipple, and then the other.

She moaned, and inside the needy sound she heard his voice. *I'm trying to stay civilized.*

Don't, she answered.

His touch grew rougher then, and her responses were just as frantic. He kissed and bit her all over. Each pinprick of pain that followed the soft brush of lips brought her a flash of mounting pleasure.

The contrast was maddening. Wonderful.

With each flash, the heat pooling in her belly grew and spread until the orgasms became one long, continuous wave of ecstasy. She didn't think it could get better—until he was inside her, filling her with hard, fast strokes that drowned her in fiery sensation. She clung to him, rose to meet him with the same frantic energy, wanted nothing but more.

More was what he gave her. She gave herself up to him, blended with him, blood, mind and soul, and he gave himself to her. She was complete with him, whole with him, until one last, shattering explosion sent her over the edge and into darkness.

"That was—" Phillipa sighed, unable to describe the experience. Now she understood why sex was called The Little Death. Maybe only good sex was called that. Great sex.

Little sparks of pleasure were still shooting through her. She was exhilarated and exhausted at the same time. She was completely content to come back to reality to find herself lying across

Matt, with her breasts pressed against the hard muscles of his bare chest. She rested her cheek against the warmth of his skin, and breathed in his male scent.

"It certainly was," Matt answered.

He was lying on a pile of pillows, his hands propped behind his head, a smug smile curving his beautiful mouth. She caught the sparkle of green in his half-closed eyes.

"You look like a well-fed cat," she told him.

"Very well-fed," he answered. "But still hungry."

He pulled her up the length of his body for a kiss. His mouth was as insistent and needy as if they hadn't just made love. As his hands began to roam, he made her hungry all over again.

This time she was able to keep her head long enough to say, "Maybe we shouldn't." His mouth circled a nipple. "Oh, God! I mean— there's supposed to be photos—and—wedding stuff." She was too deep into the pleasure to remember just what. "We'll be missed."

He nuzzled her, and his voice was muffled from between her breasts. "Do you really care?"

"Nooo—yes! We'll be missed. I should be there. She's my sis—" She suddenly became very aware of his erection, and her hand closed around it. She had to touch him, to stroke him. "I shouldn't be doing this."

"You better not stop."

His hungry growl sent a needy shiver through

her. His voice was enough to make her melt. "But—"

This sort of thing happens at family gatherings all the time.

"What happens?"

People disappear to make love. It's a way to celebrate the bonding.

"That's nice." It occurred to Phillipa that there was something odd about this conversation. "Did you just say something inside my head?"

Not that you'll recall. Relax, sweetness. Make love to me.

"All right." It was all she wanted to do anyway.

A carousel music version of "Ode to Joy" woke Phillipa up, but her first thought was, *I belong with this man.* When she came a little further awake she realized that the noise was a cell phone ringing, and that she was lying naked in a dark hotel room with Matt Bridger. She couldn't think of anywhere better to be, and snuggled closer to him while Beethoven kept playing.

Eventually Matt grunted and rolled over to pick the phone up from the nightstand. "Mike, if you're drunk, you're a dead lobo." Whatever the answer was, it made Matt sit up. His muscles bunched with tension. "Where and when? Right. I'm not alone."

Phillipa decided to let him ride out this emergency in privacy, and took the opportunity to slide out of bed for the bathroom. She took her time using the facilities and drinking a glass of water.

As she stepped back into the dark bedroom she was aware of its emptiness. The musky tang of sex was still in the air—but even before she turned on a light and saw the rumpled, empty bed, she knew he was gone.